MIYA'S DREAM

DREAM

Cathy Ringler

Crystal Publishing LLC
Fort Collins, Colorado

MIYA'S DREAM

2019 © COPYRIGHT Cathy Ringler
2019 © COVER COPYRIGHT Crystal Publishing, LLC

Edited by Lindsey Maugham, Keri De Deo, Malory Wood, Claire Shepherd, and Patricia Phillips

Cover design by lotusdesign.biz
Art by Tawni Shuler

Published by Crystal Publishing, LLC
Fort Collins, Colorado

ISBN 978-1-942624-58-5
Library of Congress Control Number: 2019935647

To Stetson, Denali, and Ryder:
my three favorite cowkids.

Chapter One

Miya's dad drove under the iron archway and pulled into the barnyard.

"Number 31. This must be the place." The truck clanked to a stop, and grease-stained fingers turned off the ignition. While he unbuckled his seatbelt, he winked at Miya. "Today is the day we'll find your dream horse."

Miya hoped so. This horse, Dragon, had been advertised online. The ad said the owner's daughter had won several barrel races on him, but now she had new interests. Miya stared at the gleaming white fence and freshly painted red barn. Pretty fancy, especially when compared with the old wooden corrals at Miya's house.

A man and two girls came out of the barn. Miya watched them approach. She didn't recognize the man, but she knew the girls: Skylar Peters and Ella Anderson. Everybody knew Skylar and Ella because they were on the volleyball team, dance team, student council, and a bunch of other stuff. You name it, they were in on it.

The pair looked enough alike to be related, rather than just joined at the hip. Thin. Tan. Blond. Rockstar cowgirl jeans with sparkly back pockets. Miya sighed. She would kill for a pair of Rockstars.

She had never actually talked to the two since she rarely crossed paths with the popular kids. But who knew? Maybe they were nice.

The man and the girls came over to the truck. The Carhart coat he wore looked brand new and stiff—not a single stain or barbed wire rip.

As they approached, Dad leaned out the window. "Hi, I'm Thomas Skippingbird. This is my daughter, Miya. We've come to look at your barrel horse."

The man reached into the truck, and they shook hands. "Mike Peters here. This is my daughter, Skylar, and her friend, Ella."

Skylar spoke up, "Dad, we know Miya from school."

"Oh. Good, then," Mike said. "Let's head out to the barn. The trainer has Dragon saddled."

Dad waited, his hand hovering near the gear shift. "Should I pull closer to the barn?"

"You know . . ." Mike paused and studied their trailer. "People are coming out later for a clinic. Why don't you drive your rig around back? That way there will be plenty of room for everyone to park. We'll jump on the four-wheeler and show you."

Dad put the truck into gear. He smiled at Miya. "Let's go take a look at this horse."

Mike and the girls squeezed onto the four-wheeler, and they roared off. Skylar and Ella twisted around and looked back at the truck, pointing and laughing. Miya and Dad followed more slowly with the trailer. After he parked, Dad joined the group, but Miya hesitated inside the truck.

As everyone else headed inside the barn, Skylar's and Ella's pockets glinted in the sunshine. Miya opened the door and paused. The running board on the passenger side had been ripped off last winter when Dad had gotten stuck in a snowdrift. A graceful exit was impossible. Miya slid out and landed with a squelch.

Of course.

Dad had parked in a mud puddle. Miya tried to move her right foot, but the sticky mud gripped her boot. She curled her toes and pulled. Still stuck. If she tried to walk, she'd step right out of her boots and wind up hopping around in her socks. Miya leaned down, grasped the top of her boot, and tugged.

The breeze carried Skylar's voice. "Where did she go?"

Miya froze in place.

"I don't know," said Ella. "She could be inside with the dads."

Miya didn't breathe and crouched lower to make sure the truck hid her from view.

"I can't believe they have the nerve to show up here. I'm done with barrel racing, but it's not like we're giving Dragon away for nothing."

"I'm sure they expect to pay a fair price."

"Please. Why do you think Dad made them park their rig in the back? I think they want Dad to feel sorry for them and give them a good deal because they're Indians."

"He doesn't have to come down in price. Other people are coming to look at Dragon, right?"

"Yeah. Hopefully, someone who's not so fat. I feel sorry for the horse when she tries him out."

The girls' voices faded. Miya started to shake, and she hid her face in her hands. She took deep breaths, in and out.

Just get through it. In. Out. Get through it.

Miya reached down, wrenched her boot free, and jumped back into the truck. She climbed across to the driver's side and slid out onto dry ground.

Dad called from the barn door. "Why are you still over there? This horse is ready to ride."

Keeping her head down, she hurried toward Dad. If only she were five again, she would tell on the girls, and they would get into trouble. Miya would get a hug, and the problem would go away. Except it wouldn't. She knew from experience that

3

the words "fat," "poor," and "Indian" would stay written on her heart in permanent marker.

Miya stepped into the barn while Skylar and Ella sat in the bleachers, scrolling through their phones and giggling. Miya turned away from them and breathed in the familiar smell of horses and hay. The trainer, a middle-aged woman in a black down vest, smiled at her. "Hi, I'm Judy. This is Dragon."

For a minute, Miya stared at the horse. If she could choose the perfect barrel prospect, it would be Dragon—a glistening sorrel with a white blaze down his nose and three white socks. Miya took a step forward and rubbed his neck. He turned to look at her with dark chocolate eyes, tossing his head and pawing with nervous energy.

"You are gorgeous," Miya whispered to him.

"Ready?" Judy asked.

She led him out to the arena and over to a mounting block. Miya settled into the saddle, picked up her reins, and the world fell away. She and Dragon walked, trotted, and loped circles. No, they floated in beautiful circles. She couldn't wipe the grin off her face. Miya rocked gently back and forth with his gait, her braid tapping her back with each stride.

She'd never ridden a horse like Dragon. He responded to her lightest cues. Miya only had to think about telling him to step over before he did it.

The trainer's voice brought her back to reality. "Miya, would you like to take him around the barrels?"

Would she ever!

Miya rode Dragon into the alley and stopped to settle him down a bit. She planned to trot the pattern the first time and then lope it. As they headed into the arena, however, Dragon's muscles bunched with anticipation, and he pulled at the bit.

Miya patted his neck. "You want to make a rodeo run, huh? Your best, fastest run? Let's do it." She loosened the reins, sat forward in the saddle, and time exploded.

Dragon raced to the first barrel, turned perfectly, and came out of the turn hard. Miya gripped the saddle horn to stay in position. He flew to the second barrel, made another tight turn, and before she knew it, he rounded the third. Dragon stretched out as he ran home.

Miya's heart pounded as she slipped off and loosened his cinch. "Wow, they should have named you Pegasus."

Miya didn't want to let him go. With Dragon prancing beside her, she walked back through the arena sand to where the others waited. The joy she'd felt a moment ago turned cold and hard in her stomach. Her family could never afford him. If only she had a horse like Dragon, she wouldn't be afraid to enter barrel races. People would be so busy watching him, they'd never notice her fat rolls.

She stopped beside Dad. He glanced at her with a brief smile before he turned back to the registration papers.

"He's a beautiful horse. You can't fault his bloodlines."

Mike nodded. "Yep. He's well bred."

Miya looked down. Mike's boots didn't have a single scuff mark, not even on the toes.

"How much are you asking for him?"

Miya crossed her fingers, her toes, her eyes.

Please let there be a miracle. Say $3,500. Say $3,500.

Skylar and Ella stood beside Mike, pretending to be engrossed in their cellphones, all the while glancing sideways at Miya and smirking.

Mike shifted in his new boots. "We bought him for $20,000, and since my daughter isn't interested anymore, I could let him go for that."

Miya felt like she'd been punched in the stomach. 20,000. Dollars. More than five times what they could afford to pay.

Dad shook his head. "I'm afraid that's out of our price range."

A snort came from Skylar. "Told you," she whispered to Ella while smiling at Miya. Skylar stepped closer to her dad as she slipped her phone into her jacket pocket.

Miya handed the reins to the trainer, and both dads walked outside. Skylar and Ella waited a beat before following. Miya couldn't force herself to leave, so she patted Dragon and scratched his forehead. He nosed her pockets and blew softly on her coat.

"Are you looking for a treat?" Miya whispered. "I wish I'd brought one."

Skylar and Ella stopped at the barn door, looked toward Miya, and giggled. Skylar's voice floated back as they stepped outside. "Can you believe how Mega Miya was all over that horse? It's a good thing they don't have the money. She's not ready for him. She should go to the horse sale and get some cheap old horse she can handle."

Miya swallowed. *So much for Dragon.* She was too fat for him anyway.

Chapter Two

Miya picked up her phone and then laid it back down on the truck seat. She wanted to scroll through it, but she knew Dad would tell her to stop staring at her phone and talk to him instead. Miya wasn't quite ready to talk, not this early in the morning. Instead, she gazed out the window. The weak April sun poked its way through the low clouds.

Dad cleared his throat. "It's a beautiful Saturday. We'll look back and remember it as the day we found your barrel horse."

Miya grunted. That's what he had said last Saturday about Dragon. "Dad, I feel bad that you're spending so much time and gas money on this wild goose chase. It was a dumb idea from the start."

"No, it wasn't." Dad slowed the truck as three deer crossed the road in front of them. "When you start winning, you'll realize it was a great idea."

"Dad, I won't ever win!" Miya shifted in her seat and turned to face him. "We can't afford a horse like Dragon, and that's the kind of horse you need to get a check."

"Not necessarily." Dad turned to her, his eyes serious. "I'm not denying he was a nice horse. But the more I thought about it, the more I realized he wasn't the right one for you, even if we had the money."

Miya's mouth fell open. "You wouldn't say that if you had ridden him."

"Sure, I would. You don't need a finished barrel horse. You need a horse that's been started, but one you train so the two of you will build a bond. You'll trust each other, and it will pay off in a lot of places, including the rodeo arena."

"Bond with my horse," Miya muttered. "Maybe my new horse won't call me Mega Miya."

"What did you say?" Dad drove on to the next road.

"I was just talking to myself." Miya slid back down into the seat and turned back to the window.

He didn't understand. She didn't have years to spend training a horse. She needed to win right away. If she had an awesome horse that won every time, the rodeo kids would notice the good things about her, and maybe next year when she started high school, the other kids would notice those good things, too. They might even begin to like her.

A hawk flew from its perch on a fence post. Dad hummed along with "Mommas Don't Let Your Babies Grow Up to Be Cowboys," a golden-oldies song on the radio. He smiled, reached across the seat, and gripped her hand for a minute. Slowing the truck, he said, "I hope we didn't pass the turnoff."

She pointed. "This could be it. I see a barn back there."

"Me, too." Dad swung the truck wide to avoid hitting the mailbox with the trailer. "So what did you say just now?"

"Nothing important."

Dad stepped on the brake and turned to look at her. "Are you sure it's nothing important?"

Miya nodded. "I'm sure."

Telling Dad wouldn't change how the other kids treated her. It would just make him feel bad. She'd have to figure it out herself.

Dad tugged gently on her braid. "Okay. Let's go find us a barrel horse."

The truck turned into a narrower lane. As the trailer rattled by, prairie dogs disappeared with a quick flip of their tails. Miya and Dad pulled to a stop in the barnyard. A screen door slammed, and a girl emerged from the back of the house.

Good. Miya didn't know this girl.

The girl hopped a step or two while she pulled on a second pink Muck boot, and then she straightened and jumped across the puddles dotting the barnyard.

"I can feel it in my bones. Today is the day we'll find your dream horse," Dad said.

Miya shrugged. "If you say so."

They climbed out of the truck.

The girl, showing off perfectly straight, white teeth with a welcoming smile, held out her hand. "Hi, I'm Julia."

Dad shook Julia's hand. "I'm Thomas Skippingbird. This is Miya."

Miya nodded. She went around to the back of the truck, leaving Dad to talk to Julia. After last weekend, she'd had enough of perky blondes with white teeth. Lowering the tailgate, she leaned forward to pull her saddle toward her. The saddle had shifted to the front of the bed, just out of reach. Miya stood on tiptoes and strained to touch the pad. The edge of the tailgate cut into her stomach, making her wince.

Dad came around the truck. "I'll get it. Julia was saying that she is home from college for spring break."

Miya plastered on a fake smile and turned. "That's nice. Where do you go to school?"

"Bozeman."

"Cool. Don't they have a rodeo team there?"

"Yeah, and I went out freshman year, but since I'm working my way through pre-vet classes, I don't have enough time for both school and rodeo." Julia pulled on her gloves. "Where do you want to go to college?"

Miya looked down at her jacket and brushed some dog hair off the front. "I'd like to start at a small college with a rodeo team and then go to UW in Laramie."

"Good plan." Julia nodded.

9

Miya glanced toward the barn where a horse stood at the hitching rail. From this distance, she couldn't tell too much about the horse, except it was a paint.

Julia played with a locket around her neck. "Let me tell you about Dream. I'm trying to graduate early, so I'm spending my summers at school. That means Dream hasn't even been saddled for the past couple of years."

Miya shifted her attention away from the horse and back to the older girl. "That's okay."

"We just missed a national championship in goat tying my last year in Junior Rodeo." Julia touched her left earring—a tiny, silver horse. "Wow! I guess that's almost three years ago now."

Goat tying. Yuck.

Miya tried goat tying before. It was ridiculous. Miya had to run her horse, Ace, down the arena to the goat, jump off while still loping, get her balance, run a few steps, tie the goat in a crazy knot with wraps and some loop thing called a "hooey." Miya had dismounted, alright—flat on her face. It took days to get the dirt out of her braces.

Miya missed Ace. He had been her dad's horse for years. When he got too old to be ridden hard, Ace had become Miya's horse. They had made a great team. Ace was lame from arthritis now, so he mostly stood in his favorite sunny spot out in the field, swishing flies and dozing.

"Miya?"

Miya brought her attention back to Julia. "Sorry. I was just thinking about my old horse, Ace."

"I know how it feels to have a bond with a good horse." Julia looked toward the horse at the hitching rail. "I hope that will happen if you buy Dream. We ran barrels and roped some, too, although barrels weren't really my thing."

"Oh," Miya said. "Umm, nice."

"Yeah. I kinda feel guilty about keeping her here. She's too good a horse to just stand around. But if I sell her, I want her to go to the right home where she'll have a job."

Miya nodded. She stared at the lift ticket fastened to the zipper on Julia's North Face jacket. Miya cleared her throat. "I haven't competed much, but I'd like to try."

Julia's smile widened. "You should. You'd have a lot of fun."

Miya glanced around. Where was Dad? A little help here would be nice. She cleared her throat again. "We live on a ranch and run some cows, so Dream would be used whether or not I get to rodeo much."

"She's good on cows. Do you want to meet her?"

"Sure."

Dad waited by the paint. He smiled as they got closer. "I didn't want to saddle her until I was sure, but this is the horse that's for sale. Right?"

"Yep. This is Dream." Julia untied her. "As you can see, she's an easy keeper."

Miya's eyes widened. She didn't know if she'd ever seen a fatter or fuzzier horse. Dream's stomach drooped.

"She's not pregnant, is she?"

"Oh, no." Julia laughed. "She just really loves her groceries."

Miya stroked the gigantic dust bunny with legs. This horse couldn't be a running horse.

Another wasted trip.

She stepped aside and stuck her hands in her pockets while Dad ran his hands down the mare's legs and lifted her feet.

"How old is she?"

"She's nine. You can look at her teeth. She won't mind."

Dad pried Dream's lips apart. After he studied her teeth for a minute, he wiped the horse spit on Dream's fuzzy shoulder. "Do you have her papers handy?"

"Yeah, I left them in the tack room. I'll get them for you."

After Julia disappeared, Miya stepped over to Dad and whispered in his ear. "Dad. It's okay. I know you have a lot to do today. We can go. I don't have to ride her."

Dad winked, and his smile crinkled his eyes. When Julia reappeared with the papers, he took his glasses out of his breast pocket and set them on his nose. He read them over while Miya shifted from foot to foot.

As Miya watched Dad read, she noticed a greenish-brown glob on the front of his jacket. Miya blushed. Why hadn't he changed clothes after he fed the cows this morning? She stole a glance at Julia, who looked at it, too. Finally, he handed the folder back, took off his glasses, and returned them to his pocket.

"Let's get a saddle on this horse," he said.

Miya looked at Dream standing like a spotted elephant and rolled her eyes.

"You can't tell because of all this hair, but I've already brushed her. While you guys are saddling her, I'll get her bridle." Julia disappeared into the barn.

"Dad, why are we even . . ." Miya stopped midsentence. Julia returned with the bridle.

Dad lifted the saddle onto Dream's broad back and leaned down to get ahold of the cinch. "It's not long enough. Would you let it out on the other side?"

She walked around behind Dream. The mare stomped a hind foot and swished her tail. Miya let out the billet to the last hole and handed the cinch underneath to be tightened. It barely fit around Dream's belly. The paint pinned back her ears in annoyance. Miya consoled herself by remembering she wouldn't have to ride her again after today.

What an old crabby pants.

Julia slipped the bit into Dream's mouth and gently pulled the headstall over the mare's ears. She scratched the paint's head. "Quit your antics and behave yourself. You're giving Miya the wrong impression."

No, she's not, thought Miya.

Julia led Dream over to the arena while Miya and Dad trailed behind. "I got on the four-wheeler and worked up the east end after you called. It drains to the west, so it's still a skating rink over there. The ground is better on this end. It's mostly mud with a few slick spots, but you should be fine if you take it slow and stay over by the barn."

"Sounds like a good plan," Dad said.

Julia led Dream in, shut the gate, and turned to Miya. "Would you like to ride first? Or would you like me to warm her up?"

Miya flushed. Why was it always the same? The perfect girls with perfect hair looked at her and assumed that because she was a little heavy she couldn't do anything. Miya looked at the ground and took a breath. She needed to stop thinking mean things. Julia was being nice, not wanting Miya to get hurt. Miya wished she didn't assume that all the perfect girls wanted to insult her somehow.

Miya stepped up and tightened Dream's cinch. She'd been riding since she was two and could handle a fat, goat-tying horse.

She took the reins from Julia. "I got this, thanks."

"Okay." Julia shrugged. "Like I said, she hasn't been ridden in a couple of years, so you may want to trot for a while before you lope."

"Uh-huh." All Miya could think about was getting this over with and getting out of there. She grabbed the horn and heaved herself into the saddle.

Julia let go of Dream's bridle and stepped back. "Have fun."

"Thanks."

Miya nudged Dream with her heels and turned her away from the others. Dream dragged her feet across the mud. Miya kicked the slowpoke a little harder. Dream put her head down, flicked her ears back and forth, and continued to shuffle.

Miya guided the mare toward the west end, hoping Dream would wake up if she got away from the barn. Julia wasn't kidding about the footing. Thick ice glinted in the weak April sunshine. They'd stay away from the slick part.

Miya leaned forward and tapped her heels against Dream's sides. The fuzzy paint swished her tail. "Oh, come on. Just trot, will you? We can be done if you'll cooperate a little." Miya kicked harder. Dream broke into an unwilling jog. Every few steps, Dream slowed to a walk. Miya kicked her. And kicked her. And kicked her.

"It's not fair! I'm working harder than you are." Miya glanced toward the barn. Dad and Julia sat on the top rail of the fence, chatting like old friends.

Dream took advantage of her inattention and stopped. She put her head down and rubbed her front leg on it. "Dream," Miya said as she pulled up the horse's head. "There is no grass growing out here yet." She realized that they'd worked their way to the edge of the ice.

"Come on. Let's just lope a circle, Dad will be happy, and we'll call it quits."

Miya leaned forward and kicked. Dream broke into an unenthusiastic trot.

BUMP. BUMP. BUMP.

Miya kicked again. Dream trotted a little faster.

BUMP. BUMP. BUMP.

Miya's rear end slapped against the saddle. She kicked harder. Dream trotted faster, but she wouldn't break into a canter.

Miya heard Julia shout something, but she couldn't make out the words.

"For the love of . . . Just lope, will you?" Miya clenched her jaw, picked up the ends of her reins, and flicked Dream on the butt.

Quick as a rattlesnake, Dream kicked up with her hind legs and buried her head between her front feet. She arched her back, jumped in the air, and twisted. Miya grabbed for the saddle horn, but her hand got tangled in Dream's mane. Stiff-legged, the mare bucked again. The jolt snapped Miya's neck backward. She bounced up and landed hard in the saddle.

Amazed she hadn't been thrown yet, Miya grabbed for the horn again.

With the next leap, Dream bucked onto the ice. It sounded like a firecracker popping as it splintered. Dream's hooves began to skid. The mare struggled to regain her footing, but all four feet skated in opposite directions. Miya could do nothing as they slid . . .

SMACK!

Dream crashed down on her left side, pinning Miya beneath her.

Miya shook her head, dazed. On top of her, Dream lay still, her neck outstretched, her sides heaving. Miya squirmed.

"Dad! Help me!"

She couldn't hear anything over Dream's breathing. Pain pulsed through her foot and leg.

"Daaad!" she cried out again.

"I'm coming!" He sounded close.

Dream lifted her head and started to scramble to her feet. As soon as the horse's weight shifted, Miya struggled to get free. If she didn't, Dream might kick her as she stood up. Miya's heart pounded as she pushed against the saddle, but her foot was wedged in the stirrup.

As the mare got to her feet, she jerked Miya's leg up, leaving the rest of Miya's body in a puddle on the ground.

·"Whoa, girl. Whoa." If Dream ran off for the barn, Miya could die. All it would take would be a kick. A rock. A swipe against the fence. She pushed both hands against the frozen ground and strained to lift her chest.

Dream swung her head around and eyed Miya.

"No, no, don't move." Miya fought to keep the panic out of her voice. "I know I'm jerking on your saddle, but you're fine."

Dream shifted her feet. Miya forced herself to lie back down. "Okay. Okay. I'll stop."

Running footsteps squelched through the mud. Dream turned her head toward them, nickered, and took a step. The movement jerked Miya's leg, and she felt her hip pop.

No, no, no!

She twisted and squirmed to no avail.

"Whoa, girl. Easy." Julia slowed to a walk so she wouldn't spook Dream. "You stay right there. I'm coming to you." She took another step, reached out, and grabbed Dream's bridle. "Got her."

Dad stepped around the paint and squatted next to Miya. "Are you okay?"

Miya couldn't stop shaking. Her leg felt as though it would snap if Dream moved.

"Daaad! Get me down!"

Dad turned to Julia. "No matter what happens, hold that mare still."

16

"I've got her."

As Miya lay on the half-frozen ground, water seeped through her hair and down her neck. Pins and needles jabbed her leg. Why had she ever agreed to ride this big, dumb paint?

Dad turned the stirrup, twisting her leg with it.

"Oww!" Miya cried out in pain.

"Sorry." He gently turned it back. "Your stirrup bent when you fell. Your boot is trapped pretty good. I'll have to unsaddle her. There's no way I can get you out with your foot at this angle."

"Just hurry." Miya's eyes burned as tears pushed behind them. She clamped her jaw tight. No way would she cry in front of Julia.

Dad quickly unbuckled the breast collar, the back cinch, and the front one. He lifted the saddle off Dream, and Julia led her a few steps away.

With the pressure off her leg, Miya felt relieved.

"Almost there now." Dad worked Miya's boot out of the stirrup. "Got it."

He helped Miya up and wrapped her in a hug. She stood for a minute, eyes closed, breathing in Dad's familiar smell. The tears returned behind her eyes, and before she could stop it, one escaped down her cheek. She stood for another minute, pushed the rest of the tears back, and opened her eyes.

Her hair stuck to her scalp in a matted mess of mud and manure. Her clothes were soaked. She burrowed deeper into Dad's shoulder and cringed. She'd fallen off, and Julia had seen the whole thing. A fat blob in a puddle. At least Julia didn't go to middle school. She'd be spared the online video.

She heard footsteps as Julia led the paint over. "I'm so sorry. Dream hardly every bucks. I don't know what got into her today."

Miya stared at the spotted mare.

She's a fat, spoiled rip is what got into her today, she thought. She bit back the words and turned from Dad.

"Don't worry about it. I'm fine. I'll sit in the truck." Miya cringed. Her voice wavered like a five-year-old crybaby. She took a careful step. Her hip ached.

"Wait." Julia put a hand on Miya's arm. "You're soaked. You can borrow some . . ." She faltered to a stop, embarrassed.

Right. Miya'd borrow a pair of Julia's size-two jeans which would magically expand into a size sixteen. Maybe she could borrow her prom dress while she was at it.

Miya shook her head. It wasn't Julia's fault, and she needed to stop blaming her. This was all because of that fat paint mare.

Julia blushed and stuttered. "I could get you a towel to put down . . ."

"No, that's ok." Miya tried to smile. "I'm sure we have something in the truck I can sit on."

Miya limped to the pickup and fumbled with the door handle. She had to jiggle it just the right way to get it open, but it was hard to jiggle with frozen hands.

"Oh, come on." Miya gave the handle a vicious jerk, and the door opened.

Finally. Piece of junk.

Miya threw herself inside, twisted the key in the ignition, and turned the heat on full blast. She laid her head back against the seat and closed her eyes. She wished they could just get out of here.

Where was Dad? She pulled her phone from her jacket pocket. *Oh, man!*

A web of cracks splintered the screen, just like frost. It must have happened when that dumb horse fell on her. Miya panicked. If that stupid mare broke her phone . . . She felt a rush of relief when it powered up. She could see through the cracks. She couldn't live without her phone—her videos, her pictures, her messages: her life.

The driver's door opened, and Dad climbed in. "Are you sure you're okay?"

Miya didn't look at him. She knew she'd start bawling if she saw the sympathy in his eyes. "Nothing feels broken. I just want to soak in a long hot bath."

He put the truck in gear. "Let's get you home, then." They drove in silence until they reached the main road. Miya rubbed a spot of dirt on her thigh.

"Dad, we don't have to look at barrel horses anymore."

Dad slowed for the icy curve. "I agree."

Miya straightened in surprise. "You agree? No lectures about giving up too easy? About being a quitter?"

"Nope. No need to lecture cuz you're not quitting. I just bought you a horse."

Miya stared at him. "You bought me a horse? What horse?"

"Dream."

"The one I just tried out? The one that almost killed me?"

"That would be the one." Dad looked at her, a half-smile on his face.

"You want me to compete on that spoiled, fat rip? She could have really hurt me when she bucked me off."

"But she didn't. In fact, you made some mistakes that caused the whole thing."

"Dad!" Miya sat up, pulling against the seatbelt.

"It's true. Admit it, at least to yourself, and move on."

"I really can't believe this." Miya flung herself back into her seat.

"Well, believe the facts." Dad tapped the steering wheel. "One, she was a champion goat-tying horse, so she's got some

19

speed. Two, her papers read like the *Who's Who* of running horses. Three, and most important, that mare didn't move when you were hanging upside down out there. She could have hurt you, but she waited for help. That shows me she's got a good mind—the most important thing for a champion."

Miya stared out the windshield. She'd never barrel race. Everybody else would have a horse like Dragon, and she was supposed to show up on that obese thing? She could hear the whispers now. "Look at that fat girl on that fat horse."

Miya looked around. Dream wasn't actually in the trailer, so maybe it wasn't a done deal after all.

"Dad, if you paid for her, why didn't we bring her home today?"

"Because Julia's father is out of town. He'll be back next week to write a bill of sale. We'll have her brand inspected, and walla! She's yours."

Walla. A spoiled, fat, bucking horse. Whoopee.

* * *

When she got home, Miya climbed stiffly out of the truck and limped into the mudroom. She toed off her boots and headed to the kitchen. Her dog, Zoey, trotted over and bumped against Miya's leg. Miya reached down and petted her. Zoey dropped her ball, backed up, and looked at Miya expectantly.

"I can't bend down to get your ball, girl. Sorry."

Miya opened the door to the kitchen and hobbled in. Zoey followed her. Miya decided to break her diet because she really needed a handful of chips before she went upstairs. Or two handfuls. Or the whole bag.

Mom met her as she walked in. "Honey, what happened to you?"

Miya looked past Mom into the kitchen. She'd cleaned out the refrigerator—open plastic containers filled with little bits of tater tot casserole or spaghetti littered the counter. Mold grew on a bowl of chili that must have been stuck on the bottom shelf in the back. Miya looked at the black and green fuzz. Maybe she wasn't *that* hungry. Even for chips.

"I got bucked off, but I'm okay. Can Dad tell you the rest? I'm taking a hot bath."

Mom squeezed her shoulder. "Sweetheart, I'm sorry." Her eyes swept over Miya, stopping at her face. "If you're sure you're okay . . ." She hesitated. "Go take a bath." She hugged her gently and whispered, "Love you. Call me if you need me."

Miya plodded up the stairs with Zoey behind her. Miya ran the water as close as she could to the top of the tub without it sloshing over. As she sank into the steam, Zoey pawed at the door and whined.

"Lay down, Zoey," Miya called. She heard a clank of tags as Zoey obeyed.

Miya didn't move until the water turned cold and her fingers wrinkled.

Later, she dressed in her softest, rattiest pair of sweats and threw herself on the bed. Miya pulled her quilt up under her chin and closed her eyes. Zoey jumped up on Miya's bed.

With Zoey snuggled on the top of her, Miya felt safe. She started to count backward from a hundred.

100, 99, 98, 97 . . .

An image of Dream looking around at her while she hung upside down popped into her mind. She forced it out and refocused on visualizing the numbers as she whispered them.

96, 95, 94, 93 . . .

A picture of her last math test appeared. A big red 52% marked the top. Mr. Callahan, her teacher, said anyone could retest for a higher grade, but how would that help? She didn't get that stuff. She'd just fail again.

Miya took a deep breath and, starting with her toes, tightened up all of her muscles, and forced them to relax.

92, 91, 90, 89 . . .

Last Friday in gym, Skylar looked past Miya to be sure no one was left before she called Miya's name to be on her soccer team.

Miya pulled the quilt up higher. What number was she on? *Oh yeah. 88, 87, 86 . . .*

She didn't wake up until supper. Miya felt as though she'd been trampled by an entire herd of horses instead of being thrown from one. Her hip throbbed, her knee ached, and her ribs hurt. Miya wondered if she'd bruised them.

She limped down the stairs with Zoey once again trailing behind her. Miya walked into the kitchen. The counters were clean, and the plastic containers had been stashed in the dishwasher. Only two places were set for supper. Mom stirred something inside a pot on the stove. She turned when Miya sat down.

"You took a long nap."

"Yeah." Miya reached for a roll. "I've been tired all week. Hope I'm not coming down with something." She planted the seed early in case she needed to be sick on Monday. She opened the butter. "Where's Dad?"

"He's out in the shop trying to get that tractor running. He'll eat later."

While Miya slathered her roll with butter, Mom handed her a bowl of stew. Miya kept her head down. She didn't want to talk about the new horse. She didn't want to talk about anything.

Mom sat down.

TICK-TOCK. TICK-TOCK.

The kitchen clock filled the silence while they ate. After several minutes, Mom finally said, "You know, Miya . . ."

Here it comes. The dreaded pep talk.

"I don't know a whole lot about this horse business, but I know about your father, and I know about you. Why don't you give this new mare a chance? From what I hear, you two have some of the same qualities."

The words "We're both fat" rose in Miya's throat, but she swallowed them before they escaped.

Mom set down her spoon and leaned across the table. "It sounds as if you both have a stubborn streak. That should help on your way to a buckle."

Miya tried not to roll her eyes. "She is the fattest horse I've ever seen. Yeah, she's stubborn. She wouldn't move. First, she was so barn-sour she acted like she couldn't gather up enough strength to leave that end of the arena. Then, no matter how hard I kicked her, she would barely trot. To top it off, when I asked her to lope, she tried to kill me. So, there you have it. She's not a dream. She's my worst nightmare."

Mom picked up her glass but set it back down. "Miya, honey." She touched Miya's arm. "Your dad and I are worried about you. We understand that you don't want to join any clubs or play sports at school, but it's not healthy to spend so much time locked in your room by yourself."

"Have you been reading parenting articles again? Did they say your child needs less screen time and more social interaction?"

Mom shrugged but didn't deny it. "We hoped this barrel racing thing would give you an opportunity to have fun and meet new kids."

Mom didn't get it. Being the owner of a fat horse wouldn't solve her problems. It would only add to them.

"It's different now than when you were a kid. These days the entire world is watching, ready to attack if you make a mistake."

"I agree." Mom tucked a strand of hair behind Miya's ear. "It's different nowadays, much tougher to grow up. But, honey, no one ever learned anything without making mistakes. You can't be afraid to try just because someone might laugh at you."

Miya dumped what was left of her stew into Zoey's bowl. "I know. It's just hard."

She reached into the cupboard and grabbed a bag of chips. She'd start her diet again on Monday.

Chapter Three

The bus ground to a stop in front of Miya's house. She dragged herself and her backpack up the three steps. Near the middle of the bus, she saw him—Jake Runningdeer—smiling at her. Her heart rate increased every time she saw him even though she'd known Jake her whole life. While she made her way down the aisle, she ignored the smirks and whispers, the same old comments questioning why the tall, muscular star athlete would possibly be friends with Mega Miya.

Jake tossed his soccer ball back and forth one more time before scooting over to make room for her. "Hi. What'd you do this weekend?"

She shrugged as she sat down next to him and set her backpack at her feet. "Not too much. Yesterday, I pretty much stayed in my room and listened to music. Saturday, my dad and I went and looked at another so-called barrel horse."

Jake twirled the ball on the tip of his index finger. "Strike out again, huh?"

"Kinda. Dad thinks we hit a home run."

"What do you mean?" A wad of paper sailed through the air and landed between Miya and Jake. Jake picked it up and tossed it over his shoulder toward the back of the bus where it had come from.

Miya shifted her weight in the seat. Her hip still throbbed. "We looked at a paint mare. Dad is convinced she'll be the next barrel horse of the year. I tried to tell him she won't be able to outrun her own shadow. She's as fat as a pig. Plus, when she started bucking around, she fell on me and broke the screen on my phone."

"Seriously?" Jake frowned. "Are you okay?"

"Yeah, just a little sore. We're supposed to bring the horse home next Saturday." Miya rolled her eyes. "I'm so excited."

Jake started twirling the ball again. Miya noticed a myriad of scrapes on his knuckles and a bandage around his thumb.

"What'd you do to your hand?"

Jake pushed his Wyoming Cowboys ballcap back on his head. "I dunno, bull riding or chores, I guess. Don't try to change the subject. I think you ought to give this horse a try— a real try."

"What? You've got to be kidding me." Miya tossed her braid over her shoulder.

"Think about it. Your dad knows horses. If he thinks this mare has what it takes, she probably does."

"Jake, . . ."

Jake grinned, a dimple appearing in his left cheek. He leaned toward her. He smelled clean, like dryer sheets and laundry soap. "Miya, if you could get her in shape soon, we could go to the Bulls and Barrel Series coming up. The rodeo in town starts the first week in June. I'm riding mini bulls this year. Maybe our parents could take turns driving us. Since it's an hour each way, it would be great if we could carpool." His grin widened, deepening his dimple. "I mean truck-pool. Get it?"

"Ha, ha." Miya looked out the window past Jake, feeling more depressed. Jake wasn't even on her side. Instead of answering, she noticed a truck parked in a driveway as the bus flew by. "Hey, look. Someone's at the old Mann place."

"Yeah, my mom said a lady and a kid about our age are moving in."

Miya leaned over Jake for a better look. "Boy or girl?"

"Don't know. Didn't ask."

Men. Unless it was sports, they never got the details.

Jake passed the ball from hand to hand. "Maybe we'll find out at school today."

"Yeah, maybe we will."

* * *

Miya slipped into her seat near the back of her math class just as the first bell rang. Her stomach started to ache as Mr. Callahan wrote equations on the board. He talked so fast when he explained complicated math stuff that Miya could never keep up. Plus, he only spoke to the kids in the front row—the ones on the math team. At the beginning of the year, she'd raised her hand a couple of times, but Mr. Callahan's eyes had skipped over her and settled on the smart kids. Now, she didn't bother.

Miya retrieved the school-issued laptop from her backpack and powered it up. She knew all the answers on her homework last night were wrong. She tried to figure out the first two or three. She toggled back and forth from the example in the lesson to the page where she worked the problems, over and over. No matter how many times she reread the examples, the numbers didn't make sense. In the end, she guessed on all of them so she could push Send.

Mr. Callahan trudged up to the whiteboard. "A couple of you had difficulties with your homework last night, so I will go over several problems."

"Aww," someone groaned.

"We get it," said another.

The third one turned and faced the class as though searching for the dumb kid. "Why do we have to go through this again? It's easy."

Miya noticed that although the math team acted upset, they still leaned forward like coyotes eyeing a rabbit, ready to shout out the answers before she could even figure out the question.

From the corner of her eye, she noticed someone tapping on a computer. The new kid, a girl. Miya quickly glanced at her again, making no eye contact.

Ouch.

She was skinny with wispy brown hair that looked like it hadn't been combed, let alone styled. She wore tiny wire-rimmed glasses. And her clothes. The new girl's outfit screamed thrift-store-after-being-bought-at-Walmart! Why didn't parents understand that clothes counted?

The girl bent over her laptop, trying to type. A red blotch formed on her neck.

SCOOT. SCOOT.

Someone was on the move. Emily, a girl with perfect French braids, wiggled her chair over and pulled the new girl's laptop toward her. Miya sighed with relief. Emily was a fixer, one of the kids who took care of stuff, even for the teacher. Like when Mr. Callahan would set his coffee cup down. Three minutes later, he'd wonder where he'd left it, and Emily would tell him, "Windowsill," or "Top shelf."

Emily fiddled with the computer for a minute, raised her hand, and waved it. Mr. Callahan kept flying through the problems, his pen *TAP-TAP-TAPPING* the whiteboard.

"Mr. Callahan," Emily called.

The kids turned to look at her. Mr. Callahan did not.

"Mr. Callahan," Emily said, a bit sharper this time.

He touched the whiteboard again and turned to Emily. He raised his thin, brown eyebrows. "What?"

"Her computer won't work."

Mr. Callahan set his pen in the holder, sighed, and clomped toward the back of the room. Miya looked down as he passed. He wore the same heavy, black shoes and polyester pants he always did. They were too short and flapped at his ankles. How could his wife let him out of the house looking like that?

He glanced over Emily's shoulder and squinted at the screen. "Obviously, she hasn't entered the proper login information."

"Do you think maybe you can find it?" Emily asked sweetly, but everyone knew the answer. Mr. Callahan had it, and he had forgotten about it. Again.

He clunked back to his computer and scrolled through the messages. The screen still showed up on the whiteboard, so everyone watched as notices of extra duty and faculty meetings flashed by. Finally, he clicked on a message sent last Thursday. The email contained all the information to get the new girl set up. While he read it off, Emily entered the girl's name: Abigail Reison.

Emily rebooted the computer, and it dinged its way to life. She pushed it over to Abigail and scooted her chair back to her own desk.

Abigail turned and mouthed a "Thank you" to Emily. When Emily smiled and nodded back, Miya felt relieved. She knew from experience how embarrassing it was to be singled out by Mr. Callahan.

"We've wasted half a class period. Why didn't you alert me to this problem sooner?" Mr. Callahan frowned as he smoothed the strands of his combover back into place. He turned back to the whiteboard and tapped it.

The red blotch, now much larger, reappeared on Abigail's neck.

Miya stared at him. *Why do teachers always blame the students?*

Chapter Four

Miya stepped into the cafeteria, and the wave of noise hit her so hard that she stumbled backward a step. Kids yelled at each other across the room. Trays clattered. People laughed. Silverware clinked. Miya skipped the line for cafeteria lunches and wove her way through the crowd to her spot. Lily had snagged part of a table and two chairs. While sitting alone, Lily examined herself in her compact mirror, finger-combing her short, spiky hair. Miya's eyes darted immediately to the plunging neckline of Lily's top. Miya wouldn't dare wear anything that low-cut or tight, even if she had Lily's body. As Miya neared Lily, she forced herself to look away from Lily's chest.

"Hey." Lily moved her backpack so Miya could sit down.

"Hey. Thanks for saving me a seat."

"Yeah. Our sub let us out a minute early, so I ran for it."

It was so crowded this period that they were lucky to have seats. After a couple of clashes at the beginning of the year, everyone had claimed their territory. The popular kids and jocks sat by the snack bar. The debate team and drama club had taken over one corner. Next to them were the robotics and computer clubs. The tough kids sat toward the back. Everyone else filled in where they could. The boundaries were unspoken, yet everyone knew where they belonged, and they stayed there.

Miya pushed a limp fry someone had left behind to the edge of the table and pulled an apple out of her bag. "How was your weekend?"

Lily tipped back in her chair. Her toes barely reached the floor. "It was okay, I guess. Mom had to work all weekend cuz one of the other CNAs walked out right in the middle of her shift at the hospital. So, guess who got stuck babysitting?"

"Sorry." Miya ripped the stem out of her apple. "At least your little brother and sister are cute."

"Easy for you to say. You didn't have to fish mac and cheese out of their underwear all weekend."

Miya giggled. "Next Saturday will be better."

Lily shrugged. "Maybe. It's Dad's weekend. If he shows up."

Miya bit into her apple. Since she'd only eaten a breakfast bar this morning, she was starving. Lily had onion rings and a side of ranch in front of her. Miya watched her friend pick one up, dip it in ranch, and nibble on it. Lily's mouth opened and closed, saying something, but Miya couldn't concentrate. She could only think about those crunchy onion rings and that creamy side of ranch. Miya wanted to snatch them up, smell their lovely, greasy smell, and devour them.

No.

If she ate even one, she'd use it as an excuse to go off her diet again.

"Miya, are you even listening to me? Don't you think Trisha's shirt makes her look like a cow? I heard she broke up with Alexander. Probably because he couldn't stand what she wore. . . ."

Miya tuned her out. Even though Lily said a lot of mean things about people, she was still someone to sit with at lunch. Miya took another bite of her apple, but it was bruised and squishy. *Yuck.* She should throw it in the trash and get something from the snack bar. Something healthy, of course. Maybe a burger. No fries. No shake. She'd even eat the thin slice of tomato that came on top of it.

Out of the corner of her eye, she saw Abigail, the new girl, enter the cafeteria. Abigail held an orange tray with mashed potatoes and mystery meat on it—the stuff from the cafeteria line, not the snack bar. Miya winced. Only the kids on the free-and-reduced-priced meal program had to eat that stuff. And everybody knew it.

Abigail bent her head down, staring at the tray, but Miya knew her eyes darted side to side, looking for a place to sit. She set her tray down at the volleyball table. Miya swallowed.

Oh, no. Not there, Abigail!

Skylar Peters straightened up in her chair. "That seat's taken."

She pushed Abigail's tray. It teetered on the edge of the table a long second before Abigail grabbed it. A glob of gravy plopped to the floor.

Skylar wrinkled her nose. "Ewww. Get it out of here."

The rest of the team laughed. Abigail backed away right into Mitchell Stuart, defensive tackle. Miya stared. Abigail needed to get out of there—fast.

He pushed her, jerking the tray from her hands. "Something stinks around here. Is it the ugly girl? Or . . ." He raised his eyebrows. "Is it the ugly food?"

Mitchell stuck his nose into the mashed potatoes. When he looked up, his cheeks were covered with white goo, and brown gravy dripped from his nose. The football team hooted. The rest of the cafeteria climbed on chairs and held up their phones to capture the unfolding drama.

Lily shoved her chair back and moved closer to the action. "Miya, come on. You don't want to miss this. It's too funny."

Abigail reached for her tray. Mitchell turned his back to Abigail and held it higher. Abigail walked around him and jumped for the tray. He shoved her back.

Mitchell faced the crowd. "Who can answer this question?" He waited for the laughter to die down. "Are these round, green things peas or balls of snot?"

Abigail looked around the cafeteria at the wall of students. She scrubbed at her eyes with the back of her hand.

Miya felt hot tears gather in the corners of her own eyes.

Oh, no.

Lily came back, hopped up on her chair, and held her phone out to Miya. "Miya, I'm telling you, this is great. Mitchell is hilarious. I'm too short to get a good video. You're taller. You do it."

"No." Miya shook her head. "I feel bad for her. You need to get down."

"Why? This will go viral by tonight." Lily stood on her tiptoes atop her chair. "I can't wait to put it up." Once again, she held her phone out to Miya. "Take it. Hurry! You'll get a better shot than me."

"No, Lily. Stop it."

"You stop it." Lily pointed her phone toward Mitchell and Abigail and started the video. She glared down at Miya. "I'll video if I want."

Before Miya could reply, the cafeteria monitor popped out of the kitchen. She banged the coffee mug in her hand down on top of the trash can and started for the jock section.

Mitchell, preoccupied with his audience, didn't notice the monitor coming his way. "Now it's your turn, ugly."

Miya glanced from the cafeteria monitor to Abigail. Why didn't she hurry?

Just as Mitchell brought the tray to Abigail's face, the cafeteria monitor caught his arm.

"Enough. You, go to the office. Everyone else, off the chairs."

Mitchell winked at Abigail and turned to the cafeteria monitor. "Aww, Mrs. . . ." He read her badge and flashed a wide smile. ". . . Frasier. See, Mrs. Frasier, no one's hurt. I didn't do no harm. I was just saying hi to the new girl." Mrs. Frasier opened her mouth, but Mitchell went on quickly before she could speak. "The lunch period is practically over. I'll head to class." He looked at his audience. "No harm. No foul."

The bell rang. "Alright. Go. But I'm warning you. Don't let this happen again."

Mitchell put the tray on the table and swaggered to the door. Laughter followed him. Halfway there, he turned and gave the jocks a thumbs up. They stamped and whistled.

Lily jumped off the chair, still laughing. "That Mitchell. Funniest kid ever."

Miya's cheeks reddened. If Lily and Miya hadn't grown up together on the reservation, Miya wouldn't be friends with her. Miya wanted to tell Lily right now that she didn't want to be friends anymore, that Lily had gotten too mean since her parents' divorce. But the words wouldn't come out. She looked back at Abigail, back at the others laughing.

If Jake had the same lunch period, he would've stopped it. Only a jock can stop another jock.

Abigail picked up the tray and emptied it. She hunched her shoulders up around her neck as tears dripped off the end of her nose in a steady stream. She wiped her eyes with a napkin as she left the cafeteria.

Miya turned to Lily. "I'm telling her she can sit with us tomorrow."

"Are you kidding me? After what happened today?" Lily stared at Miya in disbelief. "She's a loser. The whole cafeteria laughed at her. Besides, look at the way she's dressed."

"So what? She needs a place to sit."

"Not with us. If she sits here tomorrow, she'll glom onto us, and we'll never get rid of her. Besides, there aren't enough chairs."

"She can share with me."

"How?" Lily looked at Miya's chair already overflowing with Miya.

Miya flushed. Lily never missed the chance to compare her weight to Miya's. Miya picked up her apple core. Lily might not be fat, but she had zits. Plenty of them.

Lily picked up her paper plate with four onion rings left. "Do you want these?"

Miya shook her head. She'd lost her appetite.

Lily pointed to a table by the edge of the cafeteria. "There's chairs over by the special ed kids. She can sit there. That will solve the problem. Happy now?"

Miya clenched her fists. She couldn't stand to look at Lily. "No," Miya whispered. "I'm not."

* * *

Miya plopped down in her seat on the bus. Finally, she could go home. Jake had soccer practice, so Miya set her backpack on the seat next to her. She laid her forehead against the cool window and closed her eyes. Mitchell's smug grin covered in mashed potatoes appeared in her head, followed by Abigail, humiliated and crying, and then a laughing Lily.

Miya sat up straight and opened her eyes. It would be all over the Internet tonight. How could Abigail get past a day as miserable as this one? Miya's cheeks burned as she thought of her cowardice. Why hadn't she done something?

Two younger boys wrestled in the seat behind her. They laughed and kicked the back of her seat as they tried to throw each other into the aisle.

Miya turned around. "Could you stop kicking my seat, please?"

They stopped. The bigger one sat on top of the smaller one. "Okay," they said together.

Miya turned back around, and before she could count to five, the wrestling and kicking resumed. She shook her head while the driver started the bus. It lurched forward in a cloud of diesel fumes.

Miya knew the right thing to do. Since kindergarten, she'd been to at least fifteen anti-bullying assemblies. All the same. The speaker would run into the gym as music blasted. He'd wave, and kids would cheer. Then, the speaker, usually a cool-looking black guy with a shaved head, would tell his story about how he was bullied at school. The girls would cry, and the boys would look at their feet.

Miya remembered last semester's assembly. The whole school had stood and taken the anti-bullying pledge. The teachers, the principal, and the students put their hands over their hearts and repeated, "If you see someone being bullied, Step up. Say no."

Step up. Say no.

Even the bullies had taken the pledge. Then, like usual, music blared, everyone clapped, and the speaker ran out of the gym. Later, the teachers handed out pencils stamped with *STEP UP. SAY NO.* And, like usual, no one did.

The bus belched black smoke as it climbed the hill to Miya's stop. Mr. Callahan took the Step-Up-Say-No Pledge, and he bullied Abigail when he acted like she was at fault, not him. What would have happened if Miya had stepped up to Mr. Callahan? Especially since she was failing math? If Miya had stepped up in the cafeteria today, she'd be the one wearing mashed potatoes.

When the bus stopped, Miya picked up her backpack and walked down the aisle. Her hip still hurt from falling off that dumb Dream horse. She limped down the stairs. As Miya stepped off, she looked out at the purple-blue mountains. She jumped in surprise as Zoey bounded out of a dry irrigation ditch, tail waving and a stick in her mouth.

"Hi, girlie." Miya dropped to her knees and hugged Zoey. She threw the stick and watched Zoey scramble into the sagebrush after it. Picking up her backpack, Miya started toward the house. Zoey ran back to Miya with a longer stick in her mouth. Miya eased herself down on the ground next to the driveway. "I'll throw your stick in a minute," she said, drawing her knees up to her chin.

Zoey crowded close against Miya's side. She buried her face in Zoey's neck. "Zoey, do you think I deserve the nickname Mega Miya?"

Zoey pulled back, huffed, and cocked her head. Her ears stood up as she gazed back at Miya. Miya smiled, but it didn't last. "You don't think so? Well, me neither." Miya sighed. "Do you remember in sixth grade when I didn't want to be in that stupid track meet? But I had to participate if I wanted to pass PE, so I signed up for the long jump, but they made me do the shot put."

Zoey lay down and rested her head on her front legs. Miya continued, "Of course, I'm strong. Right? You've seen me lift bales and sacks of feed. I didn't mean to beat all the boys. I just wanted to throw the stupid thing and get my turn over with."

Miya scratched behind Zoey's ears, and Zoey licked her hand with a long, pink tongue. Miya wiped the dog slobber on her jeans. "When I realized I had won, I tried to get Mom to leave before the awards, but she said, 'Nonsense, you should be proud of yourself.' Kiefer, that little math wimp, shouted 'Hey, Mega Miya' when I went up to get the ribbon. He was probably jealous cuz he didn't even place. That nickname caught on in a big hurry. After all this time, you'd think they'd forget about it. Even if I am fat."

Zoey jumped up and nosed the stick closer to Miya.

"Fine, fine," Miya said. After throwing the stick back into the sagebrush, Miya rose to her feet and walked toward the house.

The screen door slammed behind her as she stepped into the mudroom. Miya stopped and sniffed. Something smelled so warm and buttery that her stomach churned. Mom should be in town working at the dentist's office, not baking something to tempt Miya.

Mom poked her head out of the kitchen, a smudge of flour ran along the side of her nose. "Hi, honey. Want some banana bread?" She hugged Miya.

Miya's stomach growled. She hesitated. She needed to be strong. This was the first day of her diet, and she'd only eaten a power bar and an apple. The stale, miniature Snickers bar stuck in the back of her locker didn't count.

Plus, it had been such a horrible day . . .

But her diet . . .

One slice couldn't hurt.

"Okay. Thanks. No butter, though. What are you doing home?"

Mom set the warm loaf on the cutting board. "Remember, I told you last week that Shelia Watkins and I traded days so she could visit her mother in Denver."

Miya nodded. She went to the sink to wash her hands. The sink was filled with sudsy water and beaters, bowls, and pans —the evidence of Mom's hard work.

"It actually worked out well. A woman and her granddaughter just moved into the old Mann place. I made a couple of loaves of banana bread for them so you and I can go introduce ourselves. I hear the granddaughter is about your age." Mom hummed to herself as she found the bread knife, cut a piece of banana bread, and handed it to Miya.

Miya stared at the little brown flecks in the golden slice. She had been looking forward to watching videos on her phone and forgetting about lunch and math and school. That wouldn't happen if she had to visit Abigail. She wasn't selfish. She was considerate. Abigail probably wouldn't want to see her and be reminded of school, either.

"Actually, the new girl's in my math class. Her name is Abigail. I already kinda know her, and since I have tons of homework, I better not go with you today. I'll text her and have her over sometime."

Mom picked up a basket with two loaves of banana bread wrapped in foil. She dusted off the front of her shirt. "You can take half an hour out of your busy schedule to welcome a new neighbor." She nodded at Miya's snack. "You can eat that on the way."

Miya looked back to see Zoey slowly circling the kitchen, licking up crumbs. She glanced at Miya and barked. Miya noticed a smudge of flour along the side of her dog's nose in the exact same spot as Mom's.

Chapter Five

They pulled up in front of the old Mann place and parked next to an ancient pickup. Miya's family's vehicles were old, but at least their doors were painted the same color. She hoped for Abigail's sake that her grandma didn't drive her to school much.

The front door opened, and a gray-haired lady hobbled out on a cane. She wore blue jeans and a red flannel shirt with the sleeves rolled up to the elbows.

Miya, while unhooking her seatbelt, watched the lady navigate the step. Leaning into Mom, Miya whispered, "That is the tiniest grownup I've ever seen."

Mom grabbed the basket. "I'd say she's under five feet and probably weighs less than a hundred pounds. C'mon. Let's go say hi."

Miya glanced around for Abigail and felt a flash of relief when she didn't see her. Probably upstairs in her room watching online videos.

Mom slid out of the truck. "Hi, I'm Deena Skippingbird, and this is my daughter, Miya. We live up the road about half a mile. We brought you some banana bread. Hope no one's allergic to nuts around here."

Their new neighbor stopped and gripped her cane more firmly. "Hello. I'm Lisa Reison. Banana bread sounds lovely. Won't you come in?" Without waiting for an answer, she slowly began to pivot around her cane.

Miya and Mom matched their steps to Lisa's. Mom chatted about garbage pick-up, doctors, and Internet service while Miya studied the older woman. Wrinkles and lines crisscrossed Lisa's face. She wore an intricately beaded belt depicting horses running toward a sunrise. Or maybe a sunset. But more interesting than the beading was Lisa's silver buckle. Not just any buckle—a national finals rodeo buckle for barrel racing.

Miya felt like an elephant next to a mouse. She sped up to walk a little in front and not risk bumping into her.

"Did you win that buckle?" Miya blushed, realizing she had spoken aloud.

Lisa looked up at Miya. "Yes, I won it quite a few years and a couple of horse wrecks ago. Are you interested in rodeo?"

Mom jumped in before Miya could answer. "Miya is a barrel racer. Her father just bought her a horse. They're picking it up Saturday."

Mom always exaggerated Miya's accomplishments. Like the time she called the whole extended family when Miya won the Sunshine Award in kindergarten. Mom didn't understand that all the students got a turn to win the award, and Miya was one of the last kids who got to wear the oversized sunglasses for the day. She won it just ahead of Timothy Talkman, who still wet his pants.

Miya bit her tongue. She was not a barrel racer. She owned a black and white tank. Miya thought about her bus conversation with Jake and decided that maybe, just maybe, if she could get Dream into shape, and if it turned out that she had some speed, she'd maybe, just maybe, get up the nerve to enter a barrel race by the end of the summer.

Lisa cleared her throat. "I have a mare, the granddaughter of the horse I rode in the finals. She's mostly a brood mare now, but she's had several nice foals. I still have one of her babies. Although he's five, not a baby anymore. We call him Sprint. I'll have my granddaughter take you out to see them. I think she's up in her room doing homework."

Mom beamed. Miya could practically see Mom mentally patting herself on the back for finding her daughter a friend. If

Miya didn't do something quickly, Mom would set up a playdate like she did when Miya was five.

"Sure. I'd love to see them." Miya had hoped to avoid Abigail, but that wasn't happening now.

They finally reached the house. The siding had faded to an olive green, and a solitary brown shutter banged against the wall. Two rickety wooden steps led to the door. Lisa gripped the handrail and started to pull herself up.

"Can I help you?" Mom offered her arm.

"Thank you. The darn rail is full of splinters." Lisa gripped Mom's arm, and the two mounted the steps.

The door opened up into the living area. Two chairs and a stained couch were grouped in front of a chipped entertainment center. In the middle sat the oldest, fattest television Miya had ever seen. A thin layer of orange indoor/outdoor carpet covered the floor.

"Abby! Abigail!" Miya jumped. Lisa's voice blasted as loud as the announcer at the rodeo. "Come down, please. We have company."

No answer. Lisa waited a minute and pounded her cane on the first step. "Abigail, come down." She turned to Miya and Mom. "She's probably listening to her music. She says it helps her concentrate, but I don't know how."

Miya almost offered to go up when Abigail appeared on the landing. She held onto the railing and peered down at them.

"Abby, come meet our company. These are the Skippingbirds, Deena and Miya."

Abigail clattered down the steps. She smiled at Mom and held out her hand. "Nice to meet you."

Then, she turned to Miya. "Hi."

Miya studied Abigail. No red eyes. No trace of tears on her cheeks. She didn't look like she'd been crying, which is what

Miya would have been doing in her shoes. "Were you working on your math homework?"

"Yeah. The problems were easy, but I couldn't get the stupid thing to send."

Miya snorted. "Probably because you got the broken computer from the back of the cupboard."

"Maybe."

Lisa eased herself into a chair. "Won't you sit down?" she asked Mom.

"Sure. Let me put this banana bread in the kitchen, and I'll be back." Mom headed toward the door.

"Abby," said Lisa, "Miya is a barrel racer. Would you please take her out and show her Foxy and Sprint?"

"Okay. Come on." Abigail disappeared out the door, and Miya followed.

They walked down a rocky dirt path toward some weathered, gray corrals. Orange baling twine tied some of the rails to the post. Behind the corral and pasture, mountains rose, breaking up the otherwise flat terrain. They were the perfect blend of blue and purple, dotted with snow-covered pines.

Abigail seemed different here than at school. She wasn't as awkward. Miya's steps slowed as she searched for the right words. She wanted to say she was sorry. Sorry for Abigail's day. Sorry for her own day. Sorry that she didn't stand up, speak up. The words tangled into a sticky lump in her throat, making it hard to breathe.

Abigail opened the door to the tack shed. It had once been painted barn-red, but the sun and wind had faded the red to pink. Abigail took two halters off a hook and grabbed a few alfalfa cubes from a metal trash can. She glanced at Miya. "You okay?"

"Yeah, I'm fine." Miya swallowed. "You said you already finished your math homework?"

"Uh-huh. It was easy." Abigail dropped the alfalfa cubes into a plastic bucket.

Miya followed Abigail out of the tack shed. "Easy? Even the challenge problem at the end?"

"It wasn't really a challenge. You solve it the same way as the others. Just more steps."

"If you say so."

The girls let themselves through the gate where Miya could see two horses at the far end of the pasture. Abigail shook the bucket, rattling the cubes. The horses raised their heads and began walking toward the girls. Abigail shook the bucket again, harder this time.

The horses broke into a graceful lope. "What's the black one's name?"

"Sprint."

"He's . . . he's . . . beautiful." Sprint tossed his head while Miya watched, mesmerized. "He reminds me of another horse I rode once—Dragon. He was a gorgeous thing, too." She turned to Abigail. "Have you ridden him?"

"Ha! You're kidding me, right? He'd eat my lunch." She pushed wisps of mousy brown hair behind her ears. "I fell off some horses when I was little, so I don't like to ride. If Grandma makes me, I get on Foxy cuz she's old. I'm okay being around horses, just not riding them."

The horses stopped in front of the girls. While Miya doled out cubes and rubbed Sprint's long neck, Abigail slipped the halter over his head. He had started to shed his winter coat. Black hairs floated in the sunshine, tickling Miya's nose.

Miya took a deep breath, inhaling the smell of sage and horse. She felt her shoulders relax. She took hold of Sprint's halter on each side and raised his head up. "My dad always says you can see into a horse's soul by looking in their eyes." She stared into Sprint's brown eyes. He looked back, unblinking. "He's always looking for horses with a 'kind' eye. I think his grandpa taught him that."

Abigail laughed. "What do you see in Sprint's eyes? Ornery?"

"Yeah." Miya continued to gaze into the horse's eyes. He looked back at her. Her smile faded when she remembered horses could look into her soul. She stepped back, fearing he might see the cowardice in her eyes. She dropped Sprint's halter and turned to Abigail. "Not to change the subject, but we both have lunch the same period."

The red flush crawled up Abigail's neck. "You saw what happened."

"I was in the bathroom some of the time." Miya couldn't bring herself to admit she'd been one of the onlookers, one of many who watched, listened, and did nothing. "Anyway, do you want me to save a seat for you tomorrow?"

Abigail's eyes lit up, and she clasped her hands in front of her chest. "Y-yeah. . . . Sure. I'd love it. Where do you sit?"

"Toward the back." Miya's stomach flip-flopped. What had she done? Lily would kill her. The other kids would see Abigail carrying her free-and-reduced tray all the way across the cafeteria to where Miya and Lily sat.

Abigail smiled. "Tomorrow will be a much better day."

Miya slipped the halter off Sprint. "I better find my mom. I haven't even started my math homework yet."

"I'll go with you." Abigail almost skipped up the path. The fake rhinestones in her blue, plastic shoes winked in the sunshine. Miya dragged behind in her muddy boots.

Chapter Six

Miya looked at her phone. 2:00 a.m.

She'd been tossing and turning since 10:00 p.m. She imagined the comments the other kids would make as Abigail sat down beside her at lunch.

Emma

Look! Mega Miya's made a new friend. Isn't that sweet?

Kaitlyn

Takes a loser to know a loser.

Hannah

A fat one and a skinny one. Remember the nursery rhyme Jack Sprat?

Her room felt hot. Miya's pajama top stuck to her back.

Lily.

Lily would be furious. She would say something like *How could you do this to me? Now everybody will think I want to get to hang out with her, too.* And Abigail would be hurt all over again.

Miya's toes stuck out the bottom of her covers. She tossed the sheet aside and walked to her window. A full moon hung in the sky, and horses grazed in the field. Why had she ever told Abigail she would eat lunch with her? Miya shook her head in frustration. Maybe she could fake sick in the morning, and by Wednesday, Abigail would find a friend to eat with.

Not likely.

Maybe she could avoid Abigail in math and pretend like she forgot to tell her where to look in the cafeteria. That wouldn't work, either. Maybe she could spend the whole period in the bathroom. Twenty-eight minutes. She could do that.

Wait.

Not the bathroom and not the lunchroom, but a classroom. There wouldn't be any students to bully Abigail, and there would be a teacher, Mr. O. It was worth a try.

* * *

After a couple of hours of broken sleep, Miya got up fifteen minutes early. She looked through a pile of clothes on the floor and found some jeans that weren't too dirty. She got a T-shirt out of the drawer, braided her hair, and looked in the mirror. After considering, she fluffed up her bangs and sucked in her cheeks.

Still fat.

Miya put her phone in her pocket and went downstairs.

Mom sat at the kitchen table, drinking a cup of coffee and leafing through a seed catalog. Every year she planted a small garden, and every year, despite her good intentions, she only managed to grow zucchini and weeds. She looked up from the catalog and smiled. "Hi, you. You're up bright and early this morning."

Miya forced a smile in return. "I thought I'd make myself a real lunch today. An apple didn't get me through the afternoon, just like you said it wouldn't."

Mom took a sip of coffee as if to cover up a smile. "There's tuna and reduced-fat mayo, carrot and celery sticks, and fruit."

Miya made two tuna sandwiches. Should she make three? Should she invite Lily to eat in Mr. O's room with them? No, probably not. He would be more likely to let two friends hang out than three. Lily had other friends to eat lunch with.

Miya knew from experience how Lily's cruel comments hurt. She had even "jokingly" called her Mega Miya before.

Miya didn't want Lily to start in on Abigail. She'd probably give her a nickname like Anteater Abigail or something.

Miya slid the sandwiches into bags and zipped them shut. While she put celery and carrots into two separate bags, she looked back at Mom, making sure she couldn't see the two sacks. Miya didn't want questions. Mom swayed in her chair and hummed an old George Strait tune. Miya reached for the apples to add to the lunch sack but then remembered the mushiness of her last apple.

No, thank you.

After making sure Mom's focus was still on her catalog, Miya stuck the lunches in her backpack and called "Bye, Mom" as she pushed through the door. Zoey trotted over from the barn.

"Hi, Zoey-girl," Miya said. "Just let me send a quick text, and you can walk me to the bus stop."

Miya quickly texted Lily:

Won't be in the lunch room today. Something I need to do.

Miya slid her phone back into her pocket. Miya waved to Dad, who was busy working on the wheel-line irrigation sprinkler.

He waved back and cupped his hands around his mouth like a megaphone. "Bye, Miya. Have a great day."

"Don't think that's gonna happen," she said to Zoey as they started down the dirt road toward the bus stop.

The glacier-blue sky stretched out above her, and the morning air felt cool against her skin. Five doe antelope grazed in the field. Their copper coats gleamed in the morning light. They leaped away as Miya and Zoey approached.

Miya smiled. "Zoey, don't you love how antelope swoop like birds when they run?"

Zoey, eyes focused on the retreating antelope, didn't answer.

When Miya reached the end of the road, she could see the bus approaching. Her heart started pounding. Maybe she should go home and convince Mom she was coming down with something. Before she could decide if Mom would buy it, the bus stopped, and the door flew open. Miya dropped to her knees and hugged Zoey.

"Wish me luck," she whispered.

Miya forced herself to climb the stairs. She imagined the big yellow bus swallowing her like a snake swallows a mouse. The hinges creaked, and the door slammed shut, startling Miya. She took a deep breath and immediately wished she hadn't. The bus smelled like sweaty gym socks mixed with some sixth grader's strawberry body spray.

Breathing shallowly through her mouth, Miya started down the aisle toward Jake. He sat halfway back in their seat. He smiled at her with the smile that made his eyes crinkle at the corners. Jake took off his ballcap to scratch his head, and a strand of jet-black hair fell across his forehead. He shook it back and replaced the cap, still looking at her and smiling.

Miya waved a little and walked faster.

"Hey, Miya."

Oh, no.

Lily sat with her kindergarten-age brother, Noah. He busily drew monster trucks in a notebook. *The text!* Lily, wearing a neon-purple down vest with fake fur around the hood, looked like everything was okay. Miya realized Lily had been on the bus when she sent the text and hadn't gotten it.

"Hey, Lily. Hey, Noah."

"Take a seat," yelled the bus driver.

Miya hurried the rest of the way down the aisle and dropped down into the seat beside Jake. "Hey! Do you have a game today?"

"Not until Friday. Then I'll be free all weekend. Can I ride along when you go pick up your new horse?"

Oh, yeah. Dream.

With everything happening lately, Miya had forgotten about the paint. It would be fun to have Jake along. Plus, he could see for himself that the horse was a fat, hairy dud. Jake waited. Jake had the nicest smile and the nicest brown eyes.

Miya realized Jake now looked at her with a questioning expression. She couldn't remember what they were talking about.

Oh, yeah.

"Sounds good. Don't get your hopes up, though. She's just a fat paint mare."

The bus stopped again, and Abigail got on. Miya waved and pointed to the empty seat in front of her and Jake. Nearly skipping down the aisle, Abigail plopped into the seat and turned around toward Miya. "Hi, Miya."

Miya winced. Abigail didn't need to be so loud. Others would be listening, snickering. She forced a smile. "Hi. Abigail this is Jake. Jake, Abigail."

"Hey," Jake said.

Miya turned to him. "Abigail and her grandma are the ones living in the old Mann place. Mom and I stopped by yesterday. Here's the best thing. Abigail's grandma barrel raced in the NFR. Can you imagine qualifying for the finals *and* winning the title?"

Jake smiled at Abigail. "One day I hope to ride in the NFR. It's cool that your grandma went. Maybe she can give Miya some pointers."

Miya shrugged. "Yeah, maybe."

"Thanks for asking me to have lunch with you," Abigail said.

Miya's face reddened.

Jeez. Did Abigail have to scream?

She glanced toward Lily, who didn't seem to hear Abigail's comment. Despite the stinky bus, Miya forced herself to take a deep breath.

Step up, she told herself.

"Abigail, what class do you have just before lunch?"

"Social studies with Mrs. James."

Miya felt the tension in her shoulder blades lessen. *Good.* Abigail's class was at the end of the orange wing, a long way from the lunch room. Miya leaned forward and spoke softly. "When you get out, wait for me by the door. I'll meet you there."

"Sure, I'll be there."

"Me, too." The way her stomach felt, Miya would never be able to force down any food. Maybe Abigail could eat both sandwiches.

Chapter Seven

BUZZ. BUZZ.

Miya pulled her phone out of her pocket as she walked down the hallway. 11:45 a.m. popped up on the screen as well as another text from Lily. She stopped at her locker and put the brown paper sacks in her backpack.

BUZZ. BUZZ.

She waited, pressing her head against the locker door.

BUZZ. BUZZ. She glanced at the phone. Three more texts from Lily. Angry ones for being ignored, no doubt. Miya would look at them later. Much later.

As Miya got closer, she saw Abigail hovering in the door of her social studies class. She wore an oversized brown sweatshirt. Not a hoodie. Just a sweatshirt, the kind a little kid might wear to bed. Its sleeves hung down over her hands. Miya felt glad she'd found a safe place to wait, close by a teacher.

"Hi. Are you hungry?"

"Yeah, starving."

"C'mon."

The girls started walking, but instead of turning toward the cafeteria, Miya steered Abigail toward the yellow wing.

Abigail stopped. "Isn't the cafeteria that way?"

"Yeah, but it's so crowded in there, I thought we could eat someplace else. I even brought you lunch. Do you like tuna?"

"I thought we weren't supposed to be out in the halls."

"We won't be. Follow me."

After they reached the end of the hallway, Miya threw open a yellow door. They stepped inside, and a blast of country music greeted them. A few kids looked up, but, just as quickly, looked back at their work. Miya smiled. Gotta love the art students. She'd never seen one who turned out to be a bully, maybe because they were too busy thinking up stuff to create.

A girl in a spattered smock shaped a lump of gray clay on the potter's wheel. A boy added papier-mâché strips to a chicken-wire frame which Miya thought looked like a mask. A red-haired girl sat at a loom. A few students sketched still-lifes by the windows, their hands moving with quick short strokes.

Mr. O straightened up beside one of the sketchers. He came over to the girls and raised his voice to be heard over the blaring music.

"Hi, Miya."

Mr. O was short and sturdy. His reddish gray hair curled around the base of his collar, just a little too long for an old guy. He had green eyes like a cat that saw everything. Miya liked how Mr. O never got mad. If students messed up in his class, he invited them into the hallway for "a little chat." Miya didn't know what he said during the chats, but the kids always seemed to straighten up afterward.

"Hi, Mr. O."

"I'm glad you dropped by. Any special reason?"

"Mr. O, I know I had art last semester, but I really, really want to work on another project."

"You do?"

"Uh-huh." Miya looked up at him quickly and then down at his black cowboy boots. She had always gotten along with Mr. O. He had horses, too. When she started art last semester, she only liked to draw horses. He didn't force her to try anything else. He sat down with her and helped her get them right.

For her final, Miya had decided to go out on a limb and attempt something different. She painted an oil of Jake riding a bull. She had to keep starting over because she wasn't happy with her sketch. At the end of the semester, she wasn't close to finishing her project. Mr. O had let her come in at lunch to work on it. She found out that students regularly spent their lunch periods in the art room.

Mr. O looked at Abigail. "And you brought a friend."

Miya nodded again. "This is Abigail. She's new, and she really wants to do a project, too."

Abigail shifted. Miya rushed on before Abigail could blow it. She searched the room, and her eyes fell on the girl at the potter's wheel. "I want to make a sculpture of a running horse. And Abigail loves to work with . . . chalk. She wants to do a landscape with chalk."

"Is that right, Abigail?" Mr. O looked skeptical.

Abigail nodded vigorously. "Oh, yes. I absolutely do."

"Okay, then . . ." He hesitated a minute before he turned back to Miya. "Sculpting can be fairly complicated. Have you ever tried it before?"

"No, but I just got a barrel racing horse, and I want to make a statue of how she'll look when she's ready to win." Miya put her hand over her mouth. Where had those words come from?

Mr. O studied her with those green eyes. "Alright. I'll buy that. You'll need to get online, research the steps, and visit with me before you actually start with the medium."

Miya wanted to do a little dance. "I'll get on the computer as soon as I grab a sandwich."

Mr. O turned to Abigail. Miya hoped and hoped he'd let Abigail stay.

He smiled. "Welcome. Let me know if you need help with that landscape."

Miya stretched her neck to one side. The ache in her shoulders faded away. She led the way to a table near the computers and away from the speakers. She unpacked the lunch.

"I brought plenty for both of us." She looked at Abigail. "Are you okay coming here instead of the cafeteria?"

Abigail smiled. She pulled out a chair and waited, her hands folded in front of her until Miya handed her a sandwich. She removed it from the plastic bag and nibbled one corner. Then, she laid the sandwich down on a napkin and placed a carrot stick beside it.

Miya gulped her sandwich in six quick bites and reached for the carrot and celery sticks.

"Thanks, Miya, for figuring this all out. I'm fine with coming here. Just a little worried about my end of the deal. I'm not artistic, you know. I like math and science. How am I going to do a landscape?"

"Fake it." Miya finished the carrot and celery sticks and tossed the plastic bag into the trash can. Her phone buzzed before she could say anything more. She picked it up and looked at it although she knew it was another text from Lily. She set it down and wiped her mouth with her napkin.

Abigail looked at her. "Aren't you going to answer that?"

Miya glanced at the screen again.

What are you doing that's so important? Tell me you'll be back tomorrow.

She sighed and texted Lily back.

Big project. Won't be there for a while. Explain later.

She put her phone in her backpack.

"Umm, Miya? Thanks for the sandwich." She hesitated and took another tiny bite of the crust. "I don't want to hurt your feelings, but tuna isn't really my favorite. I keep worrying that I'll swallow a slimy scale or something." She laid a napkin on top of the sandwich. "Would it be okay if I brought lunch tomorrow? We can take turns."

Miya thought about the battered pickup and the broken-down furniture at Abigail's house. She wondered if Abigail's grandma had enough money, especially since Abigail was on free-and-reduced lunches.

"Would that be okay with your grandma?"

"Sure." Abigail picked up the sandwich, still covered by the napkin, walked over to the trash, and dropped it in. Skipping back, she helped herself to another carrot stick. "As long as you like peanut butter or bologna."

"I like both of those. I could eat peanut butter and jelly sandwiches three times a day."

Miya looked around the art room. The sun shone through the big window, and its yellow-gold rays highlighted the still-life sketches. Each drawing was the same, yet unique. The kids began moving around, picking up art supplies, and washing brushes. Miya inhaled deeply. She filled her lungs with the smell of clay, dye, and paint.

She grinned at Abigail. "Isn't this a great place?"

Abigail smiled back. "Thanks to you and Mr. O, it's the best."

* * *

The next day the smell of popcorn made Miya's mouth water as she and Abigail entered the art room. Mr. O took a bag of popcorn out of the microwave. He turned around and smiled as they walked in.

Miya lead the way back to the corner table, the one farthest away from the speakers. She set her backpack on the floor while Abigail put hers on the table. The sunlight streamed through the window and danced across the canvases propped up against the wall. Miya watched the sunbeams catch the chalk dust floating through the air. The faucet *DRIP-DRIP-DRIPPED* in one of the deep sinks.

Kids scattered all over the room to work on projects. The boy making the mask added a second layer of papier-mâché over the mold. He worked steadily, fingers smoothing out wrinkles. At another table, two girls painted with watercolors. They looked up and smiled at Abigail and Miya. Miya blushed as she smiled back.

Miya's phone buzzed. Knowing it was Lily, Miya ignored it.

The red-haired girl walked toward Miya and Abigail, her arms full of yarn. "Hi. I'm Isabel." She nodded toward the speakers on the other side of the room. "How do you like the country music?"

"It's umm . . ." Miya searched for the right word. "Loud?"

"I know." Isabel laughed and headed toward the loom.

Abigail sat down in the chair next to Miya, reached into her backpack, and pulled out two peanut butter sandwiches and two oranges. Miya ate her sandwich in a few quick bites. It tasted good, but she wished she had a bag of popcorn to go with it.

Miya yawned. She had almost fallen asleep in math because she'd been up most of the night watching sculpting videos. She learned that the process was a lot more complicated than heaping lumps of clay on a base and molding them into a horse shape. First, artists needed detailed reference drawings. To scale. Then, sculptors built a skeleton out of rods and wire called an armature. Next, they shaped a body and neck out of aluminum foil and wired them on. Only then did the artists start using clay. There were at least twenty tools sculptors used to create muscles and details like the eyes and nostrils.

Miya looked at the sculptures on the shelf. Her favorite was the baby foal with wobbly legs spread wide apart as it tried to keep its balance. She liked the sculptures of the grizzly bear and the wolf, too, but the foal was the best. Miya knew she couldn't do it. Yet the finished statues in the art room and the ones online were so beautiful that her fingers itched to create one.

Mr. O wandered over, munching on a handful of popcorn. He had some cheddar popcorn seasoning on his chin, and a few kernels stuck to the front of his western shirt.

"Hi, girls." He smiled at Abigail, who was sitting beside Miya. "Ready to work with chalk today, Abigail? Your supplies are in the big, white cupboard next to the door." He turned to Miya. "What did you decide about your sculpture, Miya?"

"I watched a lot of videos last night. After I make the drawings, would you help me build an armature?"

"An armature?" Mr. O lifted an eyebrow. "Usually a sculptor uses an armature for more complicated pieces. Why don't you start with something simpler so you can learn the process?"

Miya frowned. "I want to do a barrel horse." She picked up an orange and dug her fingers past the peel and into the fruit.

"How about a horse lying down? Or just a horse head?" Mr. O ate the last of his popcorn. "I'll help you mount either of those to a base. You can try something harder next year in high school."

Hope left Miya like a whoosh of air escaping a balloon. Miya had pictured a clay horse statue—a running barrel horse with its neck and tail outstretched, streaking home past an imaginary timer. In her mind, the mare tried with all her heart. Miya thought, *That may even be Dream one day*.

"That would be the smartest thing, I guess."

Mr. O nodded. "Good. Start on your reference drawings. When those are done, we'll talk again."

Isabel stood beside the loom, waving her hand. "Mr. O, I think I broke something." He turned and hurried away.

Miya's phone buzzed again. She frowned, and for the second time that period, ignored it.

If she was going to spend hours on this project, she didn't want to make a stupid horse lying down. In that position, no one would be able to tell it was a barrel racing horse.

"Miya." Abigail touched her elbow.

Miya looked up. Abigail hesitated a minute before continuing. "You really want to make a running horse, don't you?"

Miya shrugged. "Yeah. But I guess that's not going to happen." She walked to the trash can and threw the orange peel away. Back at the table, she wiped her sticky fingers on a napkin. "But no matter what pose I do, I still have to make reference drawings. The problem is I don't know how to make them to scale."

"Let me look it up, but I think it's just a matter of figuring out the ratios. Why don't you come to my house today after school? We'll measure Foxy, and I'll help you with the conversions."

Miya hesitated. Mr. O had said no to her idea.

Abigail pushed her glasses up on her nose. "We can do our math homework together, too."

Miya watched Abigail eat a section of her orange. Miya wanted to go home, climb into her sweats, and pull her quilt over her head. But eventually, she'd have to struggle with her homework. It would be better to have help. She might even get some problems right.

Miya chewed on the end of her braid as she made up her mind. "Okay, I'll text my mom to see if I can get off at your stop."

"Great! I'll let my grandma know, too."

Chapter Eight

A breeze stirred as Miya followed Abigail and her grandmother to the barn. The air smelled light and clean. Swallows dipped, soared, and flew up into the rafters of the barn. Although the barn was old and missing a few boards, it looked sturdy and strong in the shadow of the cottonwoods.

Lisa hobbled slowly along, picking up her cane and setting it cautiously down on the uneven ground. She wore an unzipped, gray down jacket, and the beaded belt encircled her waist. The silver buckle reflected the late afternoon sun. If Miya won such a buckle, she'd wear it all the time and sleep with it under her pillow.

Abigail matched her footsteps to her grandmother's. Each time Lisa stumbled, Abigail reached out to steady her.

After a few minutes, Lisa brushed Abigail's hand away. "Abby, stop hovering like a dragonfly, and explain again why we are measuring Foxy."

"Miya is an artist . . ."

Miya snorted. "I'm not an artist. I just like to sketch horses sometimes."

Abigail glanced at Miya. "You are too an artist. I saw the horses you drew on the front of your notebook." She turned back to Lisa. "She wants to sculpt a barrel racing horse, but she needs measurements from a real horse so she can make one to scale."

"That's good. It's wise of your teacher to have Miya measure a real horse instead of just copying someone else's work."

Abigail dropped back a step. Her hand still lingered near her grandma's elbow. When Lisa stumbled, Abigail winced and reached out for her. "Mr. O is nice, but I don't know about wise. He said sculpting a running horse the first time was too hard. He wants Miya to start by making a statue of a horse's head. Except that's not what she wants to do."

Lisa stopped and looked back at Miya. Her bright blue eyes found Miya's dark ones. "What do you want to do?"

"I'd like to make a running horse, but I'm not good at school stuff. If Mr. O thinks it's too hard, it probably is."

"Maybe he's right. Maybe he's not," Lisa said, holding Miya's eyes for another instant before she turned and continued down the path.

When they arrived at the tack room, Abigail raced inside and came out carrying a rickety wooden chair. Lisa lowered herself onto it as Miya handed Lisa a clipboard with the sketches attached. The first was a diagram of a horse's head. The next was one of a horse lying down. "I've marked the measurements I need to take. It would be great if you'd write them down by the arrows."

"I'd be happy to." While Lisa settled back into the chair, Abigail got a halter off a hook and handed Miya a bucket of alfalfa cubes. They climbed through the barbed wire fence into the field. Miya glanced over her shoulder. As Lisa looked down at the clipboard, a fat, yellow cat wound itself around Lisa's ankles.

Miya rattled the bucket, and Foxy and Sprint trotted over. Abigail slipped the halter on Foxy's head and led her back to the barn. She hummed to herself as she scuffed through the sagebrush in her blue, plastic shoes. Miya followed, carrying the bucket. Sprint tagged along at the end of the line. As they walked, he stretched out his neck. He tried to stick his nose into the bucket and steal a cube.

"Go away, ornery." Miya shooed Sprint away while Abigail led Foxy through the gate. Miya latched the gate. Sprint trotted back and forth along the fence, nickering to Foxy.

Cathy Ringler

Miya gazed out at the mountain. The shadows lengthened as the sun started to set. As the breeze gusted harder, she zipped her jacket. Abigail tied Foxy to the hitching rail and walked over to Lisa.

"Grandma, do you want me to run back to the house and get your scarf?"

"No, dear. I'm fine. You help Miya measure Foxy. Did you remember the measuring tape?"

Abigail reached into her pocket and pulled it out. "Let me know if you need anything."

While she waited for Abigail, Miya scratched Foxy's forehead. Foxy pushed against her hand, and Miya scratched harder. The fine dust in Foxy's coat felt like baby powder on Miya's fingertips.

Miya wiped her hands on her jeans. "Ready to start?" She directed the question to Abigail and Lisa, but Foxy responded, snorting and pawing a front foot in the dirt.

"I'll take that as a yes," Miya said.

The girls measured Foxy, starting at her head and continuing all the way to her tail, calling out the numbers to Lisa. After they finished, Miya gave Foxy a carrot. The mare accepted it with her long, yellow teeth.

CRUNCH. CRUNCH.

After finishing the carrot, Foxy nuzzled Miya's hand. Her nose felt softer than marshmallows as Miya stroked her. "Sorry, girl, that's all the carrots I have." She began to untie the lead rope from the hitching rail.

"Hold on a second." Lisa flipped to the third page on the clipboard with the sketch of a barrel horse. "Is this what you originally had in mind?" She held up the clipboard shakily, her blue-veined hands twisted with arthritis.

Miya glanced at it. "Yeah. You can see it's much more complicated. When I barrel race the horse of my dreams, that's how I want her to look."

Lisa studied the picture. "This is a good drawing. Although it's just a sketch, I see fire in it. I see speed and heart. Those qualities are probably too hard for a beginner to express in clay. Except . . ."

Abigail looked at her grandmother. "Except what?"

"Except . . ." Lisa leaned forward, and once again her blue eyes found Miya's. "Who is this teacher, no matter how well-meaning, to tell Miya to give up her dream before she's even started? If this is the piece she wants to create, she should do it. She'll make mistakes, but she'll see it through because it's important to her."

"Except . . ." Miya leaned her forehead against Foxy's neck. "What if it ends up looking like crap?"

"You'll learn from your mistakes and be that much further along. I've made enough mistakes in my life to know how discouraging they can be. They can be dangerous, too, because they give you an excuse to quit. If you don't give up, though, you win in the end. Sometimes . . ." She paused and smiled. "You might win something other than what you planned, and it will always be worthwhile."

Miya looked at Sprint still pacing along the fence with long-legged strides. She wondered if Dream could ever look as fit and sleek as Sprint. She didn't think so. Miya turned back to Foxy. She stuck her hands deep into the pockets of her jacket.

Lisa didn't understand. Miya would do whatever the teachers wanted. Her teachers knew what was best. Didn't they?

"I'm not sure Mr. O will let me try."

Abigail walked over to her grandma and put her arm around the back of the chair.

Abigail said. "You can show Mr. O the measurements for all three drawings. Explain that the barrel racing horse shouldn't be that much harder than a horse head or a horse lying down. It's worth a try, isn't it?"

Lisa reached up and squeezed Abigail's hand. She leaned her head against the back of the chair, closed her eyes and breathed deeply. "Do you smell that, girls? It's the smell of spring, fresh beginnings, and hope." Lisa dropped Abigail's hand and leaned forward again. "Miya, come here."

Miya left Foxy and walked over to Lisa. Lisa reached out and took Miya's hands in her smaller ones. Miya could feel the bones close to the surface. She held them as gently as she cradled baby kittens in the spring.

"Miya, the first day of school Abby came home in tears. I was beside myself. Then, you came and gave her hope. I'm grateful to you for that. So, I'm giving you some advice." She dropped Miya's hands and held up the clipboard with the running horse sketch on top. "Don't give up on your hopes. Giving up on small ones leads to giving up on bigger ones. And life without hope is nothing."

Miya looked at the sketch. "Maybe you're right," she whispered.

Miya walked back to Foxy and stroked her neck. Foxy turned her head and blew softly onto Miya's chest. Miya kissed her soft muzzle. Why did everything seem so much more possible when standing beside a horse? She could try it and hope for the best. If she couldn't do it, she would throw the sculpture away. But what if she could?

"Let's take some more measurements," Miya said. "I'll talk to Mr. O tomorrow."

* * *

Miya's phone buzzed as she walked toward the art room. She looked at the text.

When are you coming back? There are two grownups at lunch now. No one will call you Mega Miya.

Miya's cheeks burned. She wondered if she would be known as "Mega Miya" for the rest of her life. Miya rested her head on the art room door.

Miya opened the door. The keyboards, guitars, and drums of country music swirled around her. Sunlight shone through the large window. Today, it fell on a collage of shoes. Photographs of running shoes, moccasins, hiking boots, sandals, and more were arranged in the shape of a cowboy boot. Miya laughed aloud. She loved how art students looked at ordinary things in unusual ways.

She still smiled when she placed her backpack on the table beside Abigail.

"Hi." Miya slid out the folder with the reference drawings with the running horse on top. "I brought turkey sandwiches. I'm gonna talk to Mr. O. You can start eating if you want."

Abigail lined up the chalk in the box, largest piece to smallest. "Are you kidding me? I can't eat a bite until I find out what he has to say." She rearranged the pieces, smallest to largest. "Go ask him. And good luck."

Miya walked across the room to where Mr. O stood behind a boy painting at an easel.

He turned as Miya approached. "Hi, Miya."

Her heart beat so hard she couldn't answer. She thrust the folder into his hands. Mr. O studied the drawings as Miya held her breath. Finally, he looked at her. "I'm impressed that you got these done so quickly. They're good, too."

Sweat gathered on the back of her neck. "Thanks. I . . . I did all three because you asked me to, but I really want to make a barrel horse."

Mr. O looked at the top page again and scratched his nose. "Miya," he began, his voice kind. "I still think a running horse is too hard for your first try."

Miya pressed her arm against her stomach. The answer was *no*. She'd have to make a dumb horse head. She reached out to take the folder but stopped. She thought about Foxy, Lisa, and Abigail. How could she face them unless she tried to step up?

"Mr. O, can I at least try? It's important to me, and if you'll help me build an armature, I think I can do it."

He sighed and looked at the drawing again. His forehead wrinkled. "The ratios do look good."

"Abigail showed me how to do those."

Mr. O cocked his head and studied her face. Finally, he nodded. "I'll allow it on one condition: you have to see it through to completion. No getting discouraged and giving up. That means you'll be in here every lunch period until the last day of school. Are you willing to commit to that?"

"Yes, I am! Thanks, Mr. O. I . . . I won't let you down." She took the folder and spun around. Miya walked over to the table where Abigail waited.

Abigail looked up, violet chalk dust smudged her cheek. "What did he say?"

"He said *yes*! I had to promise to work on it every day until it's finished, but that's fine. I'm so excited to make a barrel horse. I'm gonna try to make my sculpture show speed and heart like a real champion, unlike that fat Dream horse Dad and I are picking up this weekend."

"Maybe you'll like Dream better when you get to know her." Abigail scratched her nose, smearing blue chalk next to the purple.

Miya snorted. "Doubt it. That horse is fat, grumpy, and spoiled. She'll never win a buckle."

Miya picked up the paper that Abigail had in front of her. Triangles of assorted sizes started at the bottom of the page and reached to the middle. "You might surprise yourself and become an artist yourself. These are good triangles."

Abigail pretended to glare at Miya over her glasses, but only giggled. "Those aren't triangles. They're mountains." She took the page from Miya and flipped it upside down. "Or, if you turn the paper this way, they could be icebergs. People can see whatever they want in my pictures."

Miya laughed as she looked at the upside-down triangles. "You invented a new kind of art, Abigail. Cloud art. Like when you lie on your back and make pictures in the clouds. People see whatever they like."

Abigail wiped her hands and reached for a sandwich. "Maybe one day I'll become a rich, famous artist with cloud art, but right now, I'm hungry. Let's eat."

Chapter Nine

When Miya and Dad pulled up to Jake's house Saturday morning, Jake was balancing on an exercise ball in the yard. He stood, rolling it back and forth, until the truck stopped. He tossed the ball into a box on the front porch. While he jogged toward Miya's side of the truck, Miya rolled down the window.

"Hey, Miya. Hi, Mr. Skippingbird." He leaned into the truck through the open window. "I gotta go grab breakfast." He faked-punched Miya on the shoulder. "I'll be back in a second."

"Wait," Miya said. "Why were you standing on that thing?"

"I got the idea from J.B. Mauney."

"You mean the real good bull rider?"

"Yep. He works on his balance by standing on an exercise ball and watching bull-riding videos. I stand on mine whenever I have time. Be right back." Jake trotted into the doublewide trailer. Bales of hay pushed up against the skirting of the trailer, like miniature boxcars on a train.

Dad took off his cowboy hat and swiped the back of his hand across his forehead. His hair stuck up in clumps. He needed a haircut. Yesterday.

"Gotta hand it to that Jake." Dad put his hat back on. "When he decides he wants something, he goes after it."

Miya looked at the ball peeking over the top of the box. "Yeah, but he gets some funny ideas sometimes. I don't think anyone around here stands on one of those."

A rooster crowed loud and long. Dad waited for it to stop before answering. "I've never seen it. But didn't somebody great once say that if you want different results, you have to try different things?"

"Jake's not afraid to try new things." Miya laughed. "He almost killed himself when he tried snowboarding last winter, but he wants to go again this year. Between the mini bull riding and the snowboarding, he might not live to see graduation."

Dad blew his nose on a red bandanna and shoved it back in his jacket pocket. "Good for him. I like a kid who tries."

While Jake jogged toward the truck, carrying a travel mug, Miya opened the truck door and scooted closer to Dad. Jake slid into the seat beside Miya and leaned over to shake hands with Dad. Jake smelled just the same as he always did when he went to town, like laundry soap and dryer sheets.

"Hi, Mr. Skippingbird. Thanks for letting me ride along."

Dad carefully backed the horse trailer around in the narrow space in front of the house. Three speckled hens clucked at them before retreating into the henhouse.

"Happy to have you."

The horses lifted their heads and nickered as the truck started down the lane. Black cows grazed in the distance. A Blue Heeler pup raced out of the barn and chased the horse trailer for a few hundred feet before turning back with a satisfied swagger.

Miya took the travel mug from Jake and sniffed it. "Yuck! That smells disgusting. What is it?"

Jake took it back from her. "A smoothie. Our coach got the team started on them during soccer. It has all kinds of good things in it like strawberries and coconut milk. You can barely taste the kale and flax."

Miya watched him take a gulp. "Kale? Are you kidding me? Why would anyone drink that stuff? You used to be the Pop-Tart king!"

Jake shrugged. "Yeah, but Pop-Tarts didn't help my soccer game."

Miya stared at the lid of the cup. Green liquid oozed out the little square opening on top. "Even if that horrible concoction makes you faster than a speeding bullet, soccer's over, so why are you torturing yourself?"

"It's over, but I'm still training. I follow a lot of professional bull riders. They post their workouts, so I used them to make my own fitness plan."

Dad glanced over. "What are some of the things you're doing? Lifting weights?"

Before he answered, Jake took another sip of smoothie. "That and other stuff for agility and flexibility."

"Good idea." Dad braked at the end of Jake's road. "No matter how strong you are, you can't outmuscle a bull." He pulled out onto the highway.

"Right. That's why I'm spending so much time on balance and other stuff to strengthen my core." Jake set his drink in the cup holder by the door. His wrists stuck out from under the frayed sleeves of his jacket.

Miya stared at a piece of green stuff stuck between his front teeth. She tapped him on the knee. "I think you have some kale stuck in your teeth. Besides that, I'd like to know who you are and where you put my friend Jake. The one who used to play video games every day and eat banana splits once a week."

He grinned. "Your friend Jake set a goal. He's going to win a buckle this year."

Miya raised her eyebrows. Jake had a lot of competition. Winning a buckle wouldn't be easy, no matter what kind of workout he did.

"It sounds like you have it all planned out."

"Yep. Remember how I told you about the Bull and Barrel Series that's coming up? Then, there's the rodeo in town this summer. Hope you have this new horse ready soon so we can both enter up, and our parents can take turns driving us."

Miya put her hand up. "Stop right there. I'm probably not running in competition this year."

Dad glanced over at Jake. "Miya needs to get her barrel horse in shape. Then, I have a feeling she'll be entering the rodeo. When that happens, I'll be happy to share the driving."

"Dad . . ." Miya started.

Jake put up his hand, imitating Miya. "Stop right there, Miya. You're outvoted. When you decide to get serious, I'll whip up a season's worth of super smoothies."

Miya looked at his mug and winced. "Thanks, but I think I'll pass."

* * *

Dream was tied to the hitching rail when they pulled into the yard. Her head drooped to her knees as though she were dozing. Her stomach drooped even further. "Oh, my gosh," Miya whispered to Jake. "She's bigger than last week."

As Miya, Dad, and Jake got out of the truck, two men stepped out of the tack room. The first man looked a little older than Dad. Miya thought his graying-blond hair, silver beard, and red cheeks made him look like Santa Claus. He reached their group and stuck out his hand.

"Hi, I'm Paul Browning, Julia's father, and you know Kevin Mace, the brand inspector."

Dad shook hands with Paul. "Nice to meet you. This is my daughter, Miya, and her friend Jake." He turned to the brand inspector. "Hi, Kevin."

71

"Hi, Thomas," Kevin replied. "Miya and Jake, you two looking forward to summer?"

Kevin Mace wore a dusty black cowboy hat and a green vest over his wiry frame. He was a familiar face at all the ranches in the valley because he made sure the paperwork done. Miya liked him. When she was little, he always bent down to say hello and throw the ball for Zoey.

"I am," Jake answered quickly. "I get to rodeo this summer."

"I'm looking forward to sleeping in," Miya answered distractedly.

As the men talked, she looked past them to the arena. She shivered, remembering the pain when she had slammed into the frozen ground. She remembered gasping, trying to get her lungs to work after Dream fell on her. Miya swallowed hard as she thought back to the long, long minutes she lay in the mud, hoping and praying Dream wouldn't move.

With an effort, Miya tore her eyes away from the arena and looked at Mr. Browning. Miya imagined him having a good laugh when Julia told him about the fat girl falling off Dream. Embarrassed, she felt her face about to turn red.

She turned to Dad. "Do you mind if I show Dream to Jake while you guys visit?"

"I don't mind. Go ahead."

Miya kept her head down and gave Jake's sleeve a little tug. She stuck her hands in her jacket pockets as they started toward Dream.

Miya's knees felt shaky.

"I know it's hard to believe by looking at her, but this horse bucked me off last weekend. Have you ever seen such a fat tub of lard?"

"She's pretty chubby."

He walked up to her shoulder and rubbed Dream's neck. Dream shifted her weight, so Jake scratched her some more.

"Hi, there Dream."

"What do you think of her?" asked Miya, keeping her distance and eyeing the horse.

"It looks like she wintered well, but if you ignore the extra weight, she's a good-looking horse underneath. When she's in shape, I bet she's got some speed. Look at her hip."

Maybe she could put the mare on a fitness program like Jake's, only for horses. Her heart gave a tiny flip. What if Dream could really run? What if there was a chance she could win a barrel race? What if the kids started to notice her? And like her?

Jake punched Miya lightly on the arm. "You're a good rider who had some bad luck. You two will figure it out."

Dream shook her head, and her thick mane flopped back and forth. Miya punched him back—not as lightly.

"You're the one who likes to get on animals that buck. Not me. Hey, what do you think of Paul Browning?"

Jake glanced at Mr. Browning and shrugged. "He seems nice enough." Jake paused and looked around the well-kept barnyard. "He's got a sweet truck."

Miya followed his gaze. Unlike the ranch trucks that their families drove, Mr. Browning's 3/4-ton-dually Powerstroke had shiny chrome on the grill guard, bumpers, and running boards.

Before she could reply, Dad called them over. "Miya, Mr. Browning wants to speak to you."

"Okay." Miya wished that one of the puddles in the barnyard would open up and swallow her. She tried to look up at Mr. Browning, but her head felt like it weighed a hundred pounds. Instead, she looked at his boots.

Mr. Browning cleared his throat. "Miya, Julia is back at school, but she wanted you to know that you can call her anytime if you have questions about Dream. If you want to sell her, just let us know, and we'll be happy to buy her back."

"Thanks." Miya couldn't imagine calling the girl with the blond ponytail for anything . . . except maybe to sell the horse back.

While Dad signed the check, Miya and Jake got a horse blanket out of the trailer and put it on Dream. They adjusted the buckles and untied her from the hitching rail. "Come on, Dream," Miya said as she led the mare toward the trailer. "It's time to go home."

Dad collected the brand paperwork from Kevin and shook his hand.

"I hope you have fun with her," Paul said, shaking Dad's hand. "It was good meeting all of you."

"It was nice meeting you, too," Dad said, throwing an arm around Miya's shoulders. "Let's get this champion loaded up so she can start her barrel racing career."

"Sounds good," Jake said while he opened the trailer door.

Miya led Dream onto the trailer. After tying her up, Miya ran her hand down the paint mare's neck and whispered, "You're not the horse I dreamed of, but I guess there's lots of people who are prettier on the inside than on the outside. I'll give you a chance. Just don't buck me off again."

Miya gave her horse a final rub and got into the truck.

Chapter Ten

Monday morning, Miya dragged herself down the long hall. The combination of Lysol and Axe cologne made her nose twitch. Kids flowed around her, laughing and texting. Locker doors slammed.

Miya kept her head down. She imagined herself disappearing into her hoodie.

Math. Ugh.

With Abigail's help, Miya could understand it a little better, yet she couldn't walk into class without choking back the queasiness that started in her stomach and worked its way up her throat.

Miya got to her locker, still looking down. Purple shoes stopped right next to her brown ones. Her eyes traveled slowly from the shoes up the jeans, past the T-shirt to lips pressed into a hard, flat line. Lily's mouth. New purple streaks ran through Lily's hair.

Miya chewed on her thumbnail.

Busted.

"Hey, Lily. I was gonna text you. I like the color in your hair."

"Really? That would be a miracle since you only bothered to answer two of my texts last week."

"Sorry. I really am. I got so busy with my new horse and my art project and . . ."

"I'm not falling for it. Your phone is glued to your hand. It takes half a second to text me." She stamped her foot. "I have to eat lunch with Alexis and her friends, and they don't want me sitting with them. Why did you ditch me?" A tear clung to Lily's eyelash. She swiped at it with the back of her hand.

"I didn't ditch you, Lily. You can come over this weekend."

"I don't want to go to your boring house unless Jake is there. I want to eat lunch with you so you can tell me about Jake. He never posts anything online. I want to know what's going on with him."

"I hardly see him myself, Lily, but I'll tell you what. When he goes to his first bull riding, I'll text you."

Lily's frown started to smooth out. "I still want to eat lunch with you. Before I put the streaks in my hair, I asked what you thought about purple, but you never answered my texts."

Miya looked at Lily's hair. "I like it. Sorry about the texts. I'll do better with that. I really will, but I can't eat lunch in the cafeteria. I'm working on a sculpture, and I promised Mr. O I'd finish it."

"I'll come to the art room, too."

Miya bit her lip. Lily could be mean, and she'd cause trouble. Miya knew it. Then, Abigail wouldn't have a place to go.

"You don't want to do that. I mean, there're no hot guys in there or anything."

Lily ran a hand through her spiked hair. "Yeah. Art guys aren't hot. They don't have enough muscles."

At that moment, Abigail walked by. Miya saw her but looked quickly away.

"You better hurry, Miya. Mr. Callahan is about to close the door. I had to bring peanut butter and jelly again for lunch, but I snagged some of my grandma's famous chocolate chip cookies. I'm already hungry." She disappeared around the corner. Miya watched her go—her jeans ugly and out of style, a little too long, a lot too baggy.

Miya turned back to face Lily. Lily's eyes disappeared into tiny slits. "You ditched me for . . . for . . . that?"

"I keep trying to tell you I didn't ditch you."

"Oh yes, you did. You're eating lunch with *her*." Lily's face turned a splotchy red. "You can hang out with your ugly friend all you want. I wouldn't be caught dead with the two of you. You're gonna be sorry. I don't like being ditched."

Before Miya could reply, the tardy bell rang. Miya grabbed her laptop and ran down the hall. She skidded around the corner just in time to see the door shut. Of all the classes to be late to, Mr. Callahan's was the worst. He took it personally when students were late.

She had two choices: hide in the bathroom or try to sneak in while Mr. Callahan had his back to the class. Miya knew she couldn't afford to miss math, and sometimes Mr. Callahan faced the board for minutes at a time . . . maybe long enough to slip in unnoticed.

Miya crossed her fingers and pushed the door open a crack and then a little more. All the kids' eyes swung toward Miya as she inched it open just wide enough to squeeze through.

Score.

She tiptoed toward her desk, stealing a glance at Mr. Callahan. He was so wrapped up in the numbers on the board she knew she could make it.

Mr. Callahan swung around.

Or not.

"Hello, Miya." She froze. "I'm glad you decided to join us. Tell me, do you put any effort into the learning process? Or do you enjoy failing?"

Miya tried to move, but her feet wouldn't cooperate. She tried to speak, but her tongue stuck to the roof of her mouth.

"Is coming in late going to help you pass this class?" Mr. Callahan folded his arms across his chest.

Miya's face flamed.

"That's not such a hard question. Is it going to help you or not?" He tapped his foot.

From the back of the room, a familiar voice called, "Mr. Callahan. Mr. Callahan."

Miya looked up. Abigail frantically waved her hand. "Mr. Callahan, that last problem you worked . . . I solved it a different way. I think my way might be easier. Can we discuss it?"

The class' attention swung from Miya to Abigail. Not even the math team dared tell Mr. Callahan there could be a better way.

Mr. Callahan stared at her, chin jutted out. "If you think your method is better, by all means, explain it." The challenge in the words rang clear.

Miya slunk into her chair and pressed her fists into her eyes. She would not cry. She would not cry. As though from far away, she heard Abigail's high-pitched voice and Mr. Callahan's lower one.

Abigail walked to the front of the room and grabbed a pen out of the holder, her pen TAP-TAP-TAPPING the whiteboard. Mr. Callahan tried to interrupt, but Abigail held up a hand, silencing him. The students held their collective breath.

After a couple of minutes, she circled her answer. "To solve this equation more easily, I simply . . ."

Miya stopped listening. All eyes focused on Mr. Callahan as he watched Abigail finish the equation.

A tiny smile played across Abigail's mouth as she faced the class. "Any questions?"

"Sit down, Abigail." Mr. Callahan looked down his long nose at her. "Yes, you may solve the problem that way, but it is not the best way. In fact, it is the hard way. Now, if I may teach with no further interruptions, I shall proceed." He turned to the board.

The slight smile reappeared on Abigail's lips.

SLAP. SLAP.

Her blue shoes tapped back down the aisle. A few kids offered hurried fist bumps as she walked by.

* * *

Miya stood at the door of the art room. Her eyes traveled over the damp paintbrushes stored in spattered jars, easels with half-finished portraits, and tubes of oils tightly capped like toothpaste. Abigail already sat at their table. She unpacked lunch and worked on a drawing. With a sigh, Miya walked over and sat down.

Mr. O stood at a table, helping several students matt their photographs. He looked up. "Give me a minute, Miya. I'll be right over."

"That's okay. I'll eat lunch while I'm waiting." She bit into a sandwich and watched Abigail choose a bright piece of green chalk. "Thanks for saving my life in math today."

Abigail winked. "No problem. Thanks for saving mine by getting me out of the cafeteria."

Mr. O walked over to one of the cabinets and rummaged through it. His toe tapped to the beat of the country music.

He dumped a base, a roll of wire, wire cutters, and electrical tape on the table.

"Hi, girls. These guys need to meet a deadline for an exhibit, so I don't have time to help with your armature today. You said you've been watching videos, so why don't you give it a try yourself? Who knows, you might not even need me tomorrow."

Miya picked up the wooden base and ran her thumb along the edge of it. "I'll try it. Thanks for giving up your lunchtime so kids can come in."

"I like to think I'm doing my bit to encourage tomorrow's artists." Mr. O cocked his head and studied Abigail's landscape. Her trees resembled green lollipops, like the ones Miya had drawn in kindergarten. He smiled, patted her on the shoulder, and headed back to the photo table.

Abigail watched him leave. "I don't think he was too impressed with my forest."

"It's not a horrible picture, but I think you were right when you said you were better at math and science."

Miya laid her supplies out in a neat row.

"Maybe I should bring Mr. O some chocolate chip cookies tomorrow." Abigail raised her eyebrows. "Do you think it would help if you baked some for Mr. Callahan?"

"Forget making cookies. He doesn't deserve any." Tears gathered at the corner of Miya's eyes.

Abigail got a tissue out of the box and smudged some of the leaves on her picture. "Why in the world does he hate you so much?"

"I don't know. Maybe it's because I don't get math."

Abigail smudged some more green chalk. "You're doing better. Maybe it's not you. Maybe he's an old grump who needs to retire."

"I wish he would retire." She pictured Mr. Callahan's skinny back turned to the class. He couldn't see when some students didn't understand. "I don't want to talk about it anymore."

As Miya picked up the wire, her hands shook. She turned the spool over and checked the label. 18 gauge.

Good.

That's what the videos suggested. She waited until her hands felt steady before she unrolled a piece of wire and clipped it off. After she laid it on top of her sketch, she

80

reviewed the process in her mind. *Start at the head and bend it along the neck and down the spine to the rib cage. Clip more wire for the legs.*

The wire cutters felt clumsy in her hands. She couldn't get a good grip. After working with them for a few minutes, Miya could snip the wire, but bending it into proper shape was hard, especially with all the joints on the legs. She straightened the wire and tried again. And again. And again. She tried taping some of the wire pieces together, but the tape bunched up and slid around.

Abigail laid her chalk down on the table and watched. She winced every time Miya re-bent the wire. "Is there anything I can do to help?"

Miya closed her eyes in frustration. How could a running horse ever emerge from this hopeless tangle of wire and tape?

"No. Thanks. I'll get it, eventually."

Abigail started gathering up sandwich bags and napkins. "The bell is about to ring."

"I know. You go ahead. I want to get one piece right before I leave." Miya snipped off a section of wire. To look real, the videos said the sculptor had to bend the joints in the proper arc. Arc. That was a math word.

Miya bent the wire. Not right. She straightened it and bent it again. Still not right. She shifted the wire cutters. She had to get the proper arc. The horrors of today's math class flashed across her mind—Mr. Callahan tapping his foot and yelling at her.

SNAP.

Miya stared at the broken wire and the rest of the mess in front of her. She swept all the pieces into the trash.

Chapter Eleven

Miya gazed out the bus window as she waited for the rest of the kids to board. Outside on the sidewalk, two boys in ballcaps shoved each other. They hooted and tried to trip each other. Kids streamed around them. The bus aide marched toward them with long strides, hands swinging. The boys looked up and separated, still laughing. She wished her problems with Lily could be solved as easily as separating for a while. Miya was relieved that Lily hadn't been on the bus lately. Lily and her little brother often rode to town with their mom since the hospital was close to their schools. It was nice that Miya didn't have to watch Lily stew in her seat for an hour as they rode the bus home.

Abigail came down the aisle and sat in the seat in front of Miya. "Did you get anything done on your sculpture after I left?"

Miya shook her head. "No. Maybe tomorrow."

"Yep, tomorrow." Abigail turned around. She pulled an enormous book out of her backpack and scrunched down in her seat behind it.

Jake appeared at the bus door. First his ballcap, next his chest, and then the rest of him came into view as he climbed the stairs. He stopped and talked to the bus driver. Miya could see Jake laughing with the balding, older man. Jake started down the aisle, and Miya felt her mood lighten. As Jake made his way toward her, he reached up and tapped the ceiling of the bus. He lowered himself into the seat beside Miya.

WHOOSH. The cracked, green plastic flattened underneath him.

As the bus pulled away from the curb, Jake held his backpack on his lap and unfolded his long legs under the seat in front of him. Miya flipped her braid over her shoulder.

"Are you gonna ride Dream today?"

"Wasn't planning on it." Miya didn't mention that she intended to eat butter-brickle ice cream topped with gobs of gooey caramel sauce and watch movies until supper. She'd start her diet again tomorrow

"You'd better ride her. We're gonna gather on Saturday. I told my parents that you and I would bring the cows in from the north field like always."

Miya pictured riding out with Jake—the horses crunching through frost-covered grass as they arched their necks and breathed puffs of steam into the early morning. She imagined Jake and herself at the north pasture. They would gather all the cow-calf pairs and push them through the gate into a field closer to the ranch. She would ride Frosty, a ranch horse who never bucked. Jake would ride Hawk, and they'd have a good time getting the job done.

"That sounds like fun. I won't ride Dream, though. I'll use Frosty. I don't trust Dream around cattle and all the other excitement."

"Mi–ya," he said, deliberately breaking her name into two syllables. She hated it when he did that.

"Wh–at?"

He drummed his fingers on his backpack. "How are you ever gonna learn to trust Dream unless you ride her? You should go home and ride her today."

"I'll ride her when I'm ready," she snapped. Then, she remembered she was already in a fight with Lily. She didn't want to be in a fight with Jake, too. Softer, she said, "Come on, Jake. She nearly killed me, and I've had a terrible day. I don't want to add getting bucked off on top of everything else. And," Miya said, holding up her backpack, "I have tons of math homework."

Math. Videos of her trying to sneak into class had probably been posted. She closed her eyes. Mega Miya looking like a guilty, fat whale. She'd never live it down.

"Fine." Jake slipped his earbuds into his ears, closed his eyes, and leaned back against the seat.

Miya looked at him for a minute and then back out the window. "Fine."

The bus left town and drove down the two-lane road toward the mountains. A straight line of barbed wire fence stretched toward the horizon. After several more miles, the bus turned down their road, slowing as it neared Abigail's driveway. Abigail stuffed the book into her backpack and stood up. She swayed a bit as the bus came to a full stop.

"Bye, Jake. Bye, Miya. Call me if you get stuck with your math homework."

"See you tomorrow, Abigail," said Jake.

Miya shifted the backpack on her lap. "Bye, Abigail. Thanks for offering to help. I'll probably call you tonight after supper."

"That's fine," Abigail called back, halfway to the door.

Jake and Miya didn't speak until Miya stood up at her stop. She slung her backpack over her shoulder and stepped over Jake.

He looked up at her. "See you tomorrow. You should think about going for a ride. It might fix your day . . . and your mood."

She doubted anything would fix her day. "See you tomorrow."

Miya walked toward the door, her backpack weighing her down. The bus rumbled away down the blacktop. Miya started up the road. Mom was still at work, so Miya planned to get the ice cream out of the freezer in the garage. Mom would notice if the carton in the house disappeared, but she wouldn't think about the garage freezer until later. Miya would cross that bridge when she came to it. Right now, she needed an ice-cream fix.

Miya passed the corral closest to the house. Dream came out of the barn and nickered to her. Miya decided to visit with Dream for a few minutes. Talking to a horse usually made Miya feel better. The mare stuck her head over the top rail, and Miya scratched her forehead. The slanting sun warmed Miya's back as the breeze pushed clouds across the sky. It smelled like new grass and budding Aspens. Miya closed her eyes and heard a meadowlark trill. The bird's song reminded her of a creek splashing over rocks.

Miya opened her eyes. She scratched Dream's neck. "Maybe I will ride you today, Dream, Dream, Dreamboat. Just in the arena. But promise me, no craziness."

Miya gave Dream a final pat before turning toward the house. She dropped her backpack on the kitchen table and changed into her boots. Ice cream could wait until later.

After saddling Dream, Miya led the mare into the middle of the arena. She tightened the cinch. Before getting on, Miya led the horse in a couple of circles.

"Ready, girl?" Miya gathered her reins and started to lift her foot toward the stirrup. A shiver of fear touched her stomach. She remembered how hard Dream had bucked. Miya's ribs still ached. She could have broken her back or her neck. No one would be nearby to help her if she got bucked off today. She might have to lie in the dirt for hours.

"Let's keep walking, Dream." The two made a couple more circuits around the inside of the fence. Miya kicked a few small rocks and scuffed along in the dirt until her stomach settled down. There was no hurry. She'd ride when she felt ready.

Miya stopped again. After petting Dream's neck, she gathered the reins and blew a deep breath out of her mouth.

In. Out. She worked her foot up to the stirrup, took hold of the horn, and dragged herself up into the saddle.

Miya sat still for a second, waiting for her heart to stop pounding. She nudged Dream with her heels.

"C'mon. Let's do this."

Dream walked calmly around the arena, her head swinging back and forth, and her hooves *CLIP-CLOPPED* in the sand. Miya relaxed and allowed herself to study the mountains in the distance. So many colors. Brick-red clay. Gray granite. Green trees. White snow. Miya smiled. Everything looked better from the back of a horse.

After fifteen minutes of guiding Dream all over the arena, Miya felt confident enough to trot. She leaned forward and clucked. Dream walked faster. Miya tapped Dream's sides with her heels, and Dream broke into a jog.

UP. DOWN. UP. DOWN.

Miya posted, standing up a bit in the saddle in rhythm with each stride in Dream's steady trot. She lifted her face toward the breeze, and it kissed her cheeks. Miya's smile widened.

UP. DOWN. UP. DOWN.

She trotted Dream until the mare broke into a sweat.

Miya leaned back and pulled lightly on the reins, asking Dream to walk. Dream complied. Miya patted her neck.

"Good girl. You did everything exactly right."

She walked Dream around the outside of the arena until she cooled off. Now she faced the big question. Should she lope? That was how she got bucked off before. Miya knew she would have to lope sometime, and when she barrel-raced, they'd have to run flat out. Maybe she should get the loping part under her belt so she could move on to a faster gait. But what if she got hung up in the stirrup again? How would she get loose without help?

MIYA'S DREAM

TAP. TAP. TAP.

Miya caught a glimpse of a woodpecker in the cottonwood tree next to the arena. She watched his black head snap back and forth, intent on his work. She leaned forward and patted Dream. It would be silly to go faster—silly and dangerous. Miya nodded to herself. It was fine to just walk and trot today.

On second thought, no, it wasn't. She was tired of being a coward, tired of always worrying about what might happen. Time to step up. Take a risk.

Miya leaned forward, clutching the saddle horn. She clucked and tapped Dream with her heels. Just like that horrible day at Julia's house, Dream trotted faster but didn't break into a lope. Miya kicked her again. Dream trotted faster.

BUMP. BUMP. BUMP. BUMP. Miya bounced in the saddle.

Miya flicked the ends of the reins on Dream's butt. Dream started to put her head down to buck, but Miya was ready this time. She pulled Dream's head back up and kicked. Startled, Dream jumped forward into a lope.

Miya laughed. "Got you."

Dream settled into a canter. Around and around the arena they flew. The pair rocked back and forth as Miya's laughter trailed behind.

Chapter Twelve

Tuesday, Mr. O helped Miya build the armature. It took Miya the rest of the week to crumple foil and wire it on to the armature to give her sculpture shape. Miya couldn't wait to start working with the clay.

Miya walked to PE, still thinking about the barrel horse sculpture. She twirled the combination on her locker and pulled out her sweats and T-shirt. *Phew!* They stunk. She'd take them home today and wash them.

Lily tied her shoes by her own locker. She looked over at Miya. Miya opened her mouth to say something, but Lily slammed her locker and stormed out onto the field before Miya could form words.

Miya ran her warm-up laps and stood behind the rest of the girls while they divided into soccer teams. Coach, a stick-thin lady wearing a blue polo shirt, asked the girls to count off by twos.

"One."

"Two."

"One."

"Two."

The girls all dutifully counted off, but it didn't matter what their number was. As soon as they finished counting, the girls joined their friends on whatever team they wanted. Miya avoided Skylar's team whenever possible. Today, that didn't happen.

Riley, the team captain, assigned the positions.

"Miya, you're goalie."

Miya tried not to let the disappointment show on her face. Everyone hated playing that position. When the other team scored, it was all the goalie's fault. No one ever shook their heads and made nasty comments about the rest of the defense.

That afternoon Miya managed to block four shots, and hair stuck to her forehead.

SMACK.

The black and white ball slammed into her shins.

PLOP. Miya stumbled as she tried to kick the ball out of the net, but her feet got tangled and . . .

THUD.

As she hit the ground, Miya knocked the ball across the goal line.

Lily screeched with laughter. "Thanks, Mega Miya, for making sure I scored that goal. Whose team are you on anyway?"

The girls on Miya's team shook their heads. Skylar rolled her eyes.

"Good one, Miya," Skylar said. She readjusted her headband and jogged back onto the field. Miya slowly rolled onto her hands and knees. Her tears blurred the grass.

"Are you alright, Miya?" the coach called from her position in the center of the field.

Miya stood up and waved toward the coach. She turned to lean against the goal post and let tears stream down her cheeks.

* * *

Miya put her head on her desk during social studies. When the bell rang, she trudged to study hall and did the same thing. After Miya finally got home, she went up to her room, clicked on her feed, and kicked off her tennis shoes. The first thing that came up was a picture of her backside. Her red shirt rode up on her hips, and her enormous butt was in full view.

Miya cringed. She couldn't be *that* fat. She couldn't be.

Except those were her jeans, her shirt, her shoes. Lily had posted the picture and tagged her. The post made Miya's stomach burn.

Lily
Stay out of the way, everyone! A moose is on the loose!

Acid came up in her mouth as she read the comments. All the kids hated her. Miya ran down to the kitchen and grabbed a family-size bag of chips before running back into her room and slamming the door behind her.

She devoured the chips as she reread the comments.

Allison
She looks more like a buffalo than a moose.

Jeremy
Why don't you go on a diet Mega Miya before you break all the desks in the school?

Rebecca
No wonder she lost the soccer game in PE.

The comments continued. Miya didn't even know half the kids who had written the mean things.

Miya stood up, crumpled the chip bag into a ball, and tossed it toward the trash can. Missed. Her eyes felt itchy, and her head pounded from crying. She gazed at the piles of clothes on the floor. Lying partly underneath a pair of muddy jeans were her cowboy boots. Miya got up, uncovered them, and pulled on the boots. Might as well be miserable outside. Shoulders slumped, Miya dragged herself out to Dream's corral.

When Dream saw Miya, she trotted over to meet her. The mare nuzzled Miya's jacket, looking for a treat. Finding nothing, she blew gently in Miya's face. Miya got a brush and began to run it along Dream's coat in long strokes. Over and over. She finished grooming the mare and started again. Miya continued to brush. Over Dream's neck. Across her back. Down her legs. Dust puffed into the air. Dream's coat shone, and the pain in Miya's heart still burned, but it didn't sear quite as badly.

* * *

Friday evening, a breeze stirred the kitchen curtains as Miya and her parents sat down to supper. The overhead light cast a warm glow over the round oak table, and steam rose from the bowls of food. Zoey lay under the table, watching for morsels.

"I know it's chilly in here with the window open," Mom said. "The smoke alarm won't stop going off. I've got to clean that oven, but I can't seem to find the time to get it done."

Dad reached for the salad. "I know how you feel. I start off every morning with a long list in my head and only manage to check off about five things." He helped himself to the salad and passed the bowl to Miya. "Do you want some rabbit food, Miya?"

Miya put a few lettuce leaves on her plate and carefully avoided the broccoli. She couldn't stand that stuff.

"The breeze feels good, Mom, and it clears out the smoke so we can breathe."

Mom rested her forehead in her hands. "I'll try to get the oven cleaned after I finish the laundry tonight. Miya, don't forget to take your clothes upstairs and make sure your bathroom is clean before you go gather tomorrow."

Ugh.

Miya hated cleaning the bathroom, but she could see that Mom wasn't in the mood for arguments tonight.

Dad winked at Mom. "Yum. Pork chops are my favorite next to steak. They look really good, too." He reached for the mashed potatoes. "Speaking of looking good, Miya, I noticed you've been riding Dream every afternoon this week. How's she doing?"

Miya scooted her lettuce leaves into a pile and dumped ranch dressing over them. "Better than I thought. Dream seems to be well broke. I'm trying to get to know her while I get her into shape."

Dad used his fork to push down the top of his mashed potatoes and poured a generous amount of gravy over them. Thick brown gravy dripped down the sides of the mashed potato mountain.

"Gathering tomorrow will be good for you both," Dad said.

Miya hesitated, taking a deliberately long drink of milk. She wasn't sure how she could broach the subject of Dream without looking like a scaredy-cat baby. Cutting her pork chop into bite-sized pieces, Miya asked, "Dad, do you think I'm ready to ride Dream outside the arena?"

Dad broke a roll in half. "Absolutely. I have faith in you both. You'll make a great team, and tomorrow will be the perfect opportunity to see how she does in the outside world."

Miya didn't want to hear that. She wanted to ride Frosty tomorrow because she knew he'd keep her safe. Miya turned to Mom. "Mom? Don't you think I should ride Frosty tomorrow instead of Dream?"

"I agree with your dad on this one. I've been watching you and Dream together. It looks like you are starting to trust each other."

Darn. I'm outvoted. Jake, Dad, Mom.

It looked like she'd be riding Dream in the morning. Being Mega Miya was bad enough. She didn't want to be a scaredy-cat baby, too.

* * *

Dad drove slowly as the truck and trailer bumped and swayed. He glanced at her and grinned.

"You look good today. And is that shiny stuff on your lips?"

"Dad!" Miya looked out the window, her cheeks hot. "I just wanted to look a little nicer for a change. That's all."

Dad hummed once and didn't bother to suppress his grin. "This wouldn't be for the benefit of a good-looking bull rider would it?"

Miya blushed again. "No, Dad. I've known Jake since we were two. Can't a girl curl her hair once in a while?"

Dad laughed. "Sure, she can. Just teasing."

Miya touched her tongue to her bottom lip. She'd put some more lip gloss on after Dad went into the house.

After they pulled into the ranch and parked, Miya unloaded Dream. Dream tugged at her lead rope and paced back and forth, whinnying at the sights and sounds of the strange barnyard. From one of the corrals, a palomino nickered back.

Dad slammed the trailer door and latched it shut. He walked over to Dream and ran his hand down her leg. He picked up her foot. "I'll put some new shoes on her next week." He looked up just as a black and white billy goat poked his head around the corner of the truck. He had two sharp horns and a yellowed beard that reached his chest.

MAAAAAA.

Dad put Dream's foot down and straightened up. He waved at the goat. "Shoo! Go on, get out."

93

Dream swung around to face the goat. She pawed her foot.

"Do you think Dream wants to relive her goat-tying days?"

"Maybe, but she wouldn't want to take *that* goat on. He must weigh 100 pounds." Dad waved at the goat again. "I said, 'Out.'" The goat grabbed a bite of green grass. He chewed slowly while he studied them.

Miya put her hand over her nose. The goat smelled like rotten manure. "Go away. She hit her hand on her thigh. Go on, your nanny is calling." She giggled at her own joke.

MAAAAAA.

The billy goat shook his head. Finally, he turned, flicked his tail, and trotted off in the direction of the barn.

Dream snorted, paced, and pulled back against her lead rope again. Her ears pricked up in the direction of the goat. Miya watched her for a minute.

"She's awfully excited. Do you think she'll be okay to ride today?"

Dad nodded. "She'll be fine once she gets a job. You'll both be fine."

"I hope so." Miya watched until the goat disappeared from sight.

They headed toward the house. Dad tapped on the door and then stuck his head in. "Anybody home?" he called.

Jake's mom, Janelle, replied from inside the house. "Come on in, guys."

The warm kitchen smelled like pancakes and bacon. School pictures of Jake and a bunch of cousins dotted the fridge. They all smiled identical stiff smiles for the camera. A mousetrap sat on the cracked linoleum floor between the stove and the pantry door. A smear of peanut butter baited the trap.

Janelle stood at the sink, up to her elbows in dishes. A cast-iron griddle splattered with white drips of pancake mix sat on the counter beside her.

Janelle turned from the soapy dishwater and wrapped Miya in a hug. "Your hair looks cute today. It's gotten long."

Miya smiled. She didn't mind that Janelle had left two soapy wet spots on her back. "Thanks."

Miya had always loved Janelle. She had long, black hair pulled back in a ponytail. She wore a T-shirt that might have been purple or maybe maroon once, but now it was too faded to tell for sure.

"Thomas, help yourself to the coffee. Daniel's fixing fence, so we can turn the cows in when the kids bring them down. Miya, would you like a doughnut?"

"Sure." She selected one from a cardboard box. Janelle always got a jelly-filled doughnut just for her. Miya took a bite, and strawberry jelly squirted into her mouth.

Janelle talked over her shoulder while she scrubbed a skillet. "Jake is on the back porch, standing on his ball and dreaming of a buckle."

Dad dumped several scoops of sugar into his coffee and stirred it. *CLINK. CLINK. CLINK.* The spoon tapped the side of the mug. "I better get Jake's autograph now. He's gonna be rich and famous one day."

Janelle put the skillet in the drainer and dried her hands on a dish towel. "He's got a one-track mind about this rodeo thing, that's for sure. Run out there and let him know you're here."

Miya stepped out on the porch where Jake balanced on his exercise ball. With his back toward her and his earbuds in, he didn't notice her. She licked her fingers and watched him for a minute. He'd been lifting weights and had filled out . . . in a good way.

Miya was amazed that the twelve-inch ball didn't roll out from under his feet. Somehow, he gripped it through his socks. Back and forth, back and forth, he rolled. Then, he took his right foot off the ball and balanced on his left. Back and forth. He stood that way for a long minute before he hopped to the floor. *THUMP.* He pulled out his earbuds.

Jake turned and saw her by the door. "Hey, did you bring Dream today?"

"Yep. She's all saddled and ready to go." She paused before continuing. "Jake, don't you think you're taking this bull-riding thing a little too far?"

Jake tossed the ball into a box on the porch. "Not really. I'm willing to do whatever it takes to win. I learned in soccer how important it is to set goals. Remember, we talked about this? The importance of goals?"

Miya wrinkled her nose at him. She hoped he didn't expect her to set goals. She had enough to worry about in her life.

Jake leaned over and pulled on his boots. Miya quickly reapplied her lip gloss and tossed her hair over her shoulder. Had Jake even noticed how long it was getting?

"Are you done with that doughnut? We should get going. We'll stop and talk to Dad on our way."

He opened the kitchen door and stood at the threshold in his muddy boots. "Hi, Mr. Skippingbird. Hey, Mom. We're leaving."

"Wait," Janelle said. She came over carrying two lunches. She gave Jake a lunch and a hug and then did the same to Miya. "Have fun, be safe, and don't miss any cows."

"Okay, see you this afternoon," Jake juggled the lunch, a pop, his gloves, and his hat.

Miya caught the pop as it fell. "Bye, Dad. Bye, Janelle. I'll take care of Jake." She giggled. "It's a tough job, but someone has to do it!"

Jake stuck out his leg, pretending to trip Miya. "Since you're riding that bronc, I might be taking care of you."

"Don't remind me."

Chapter Thirteen

Miya and Jake rode away from the barnyard and into the promise of the spring day. The smell of wood smoke from the Runningdeers' chimney lingered in the air. The air felt as crisp as a bite of apple. Dream jigged up and down on her toes, her muscles bunched under the saddle. Arching her neck, Dream whinnied a high-pitched, nervous sound.

Miya put only the tips of her toes into the stirrups. If Dream bucked, she didn't want to be hung up again. Sweat gathered on Miya's palms. Her right hand hovered near the saddle horn, ready to grab it if Dream acted up. Her legs tightened around the mare's sides.

"You're fine," she said, as much to herself as to Dream.

Jake rode beside her on his buckskin horse, Hawk. Hawk was the color of Frosted Mini-Wheats, Miya's favorite cereal. Unlike Dream, he'd been down this path a hundred times, so he walked calmly, his head low, swinging from side to side.

Jake's Blue Heeler, Cap, trotted behind Hawk. He turned his head this way and that, the tags on his collar jangling as he watched for cows.

Jake stretched his legs way out in front of him and lay back in his saddle. He stuck his left hand in the air. "Look, I'm a saddle bronc rider."

Miya laughed and relaxed a little. One of the things she loved about Jake was that he could make anybody laugh.

Dream flattened her ears and stomped. She swung her head around so she could look behind her. Miya turned in the saddle and saw the billy goat trotting down the path after them.

"Jake, we've got company."

He looked, too. "I thought I smelled something." He wheeled Hawk and trotted back. Cap sprang forward.

WOOF, WOOF, WOOF!

"No, Cap. Stay. That goat'll eat your lunch." Jake waved his arms. "Go home. Shoo! Get!" The goat skirted Jake and kept trotting toward Dream.

Dream snorted and pawed, shaking her head.

"Dream doesn't like him, and neither do I. Keep that walking manure pile away from me."

Jake unbuckled his rope from the strap on his saddle. "You asked for it, goat." He leaned forward, and Hawk sprang into a lope.

As soon as the billy goat saw the swinging rope, he turned and sprinted toward the barn, his white tail flipping back and forth.

MAAAAA! MAAAAAA!

Hawk stopped, and Jake watched until the goat disappeared from sight. He trotted back to Miya.

"That should take care of that." Jake buckled the rope back on the side of his saddle.

"That goat sure moved fast when you took your rope down."

His eyes sparkled as he shrugged. "Someone must have roped him before."

Miya laughed again. When Jake had a rope in his hand, no one was safe. Over the years, they'd both gotten a lot of rope burns from rope wars.

They rode over the next ridge and found Jake's dad. From a distance, they saw him setting a post. As he walked around and around the wooden post, he'd lift the 15-pound tamping bar, and let it fall, hitting the dirt below. After he tamped several times, he'd shovel some more dirt in the hole and begin the tamping process again.

As they rode up, Jake's dad took off his ballcap and wiped the sweat off his forehead. He wore heavy gloves to protect his hands from the barbed wire. "Hi, kids." He leaned the bar against the post. "So, Miss Miya, this must be the new horse Jake told me about."

"Yep. This is Dream. The girl we bought her from said she was good on cows. I hope that's true. She did not like your billy goat."

"I can't blame her. I'm not too fond of him, either." Jake's dad stepped back and studied Dream. "I like her. She looks sensible." He smiled, and when he did, Jake's dad had the exact same dimple in his left cheek as Jake.

Jake's dad patted Dream on the neck and looked at Jake. "You shouldn't have any problem. The cows know the way to the gate. Just take it slow so the calves stay mothered up."

Jake and Miya had learned this lesson a while back: if the calves got separated from their mothers, they tried to run back to where they had last seen them. During previous gatherings, the two wasted a lot of time chasing calves and bringing them back to the herd. It was better to be patient and work slowly.

"Sure, Dad. We know what to do. See you later."

Jake whistled for Cap, who was busy investigating a rabbit hole underneath some sagebrush. They rode through the gate —Jake taking the lead, Cap trotting after Hawk, and Miya bringing up the rear. They dropped down to the creek and rode single file, following the narrow path as it wound in and out of the willows. The water crashing over the boulders made conversation impossible. Miya contentedly watched Jake's back. He rocked back and forth with each of Hawk's strides.

They headed away from the creek and turned north. Miya squeezed her legs, and Dream moved up beside Jake. Once they were side-by-side, Miya reached into her jacket pocket and took out a pack of watermelon bubblegum. "Want some?"

Jake leaned toward her to get a piece out of the package. Instead of straightening up after he accepted a piece, Jake leaned over farther and put his hand on Miya's saddle horn.

"What would you do if I pulled you off your horse?" He grabbed for her arm, but Miya moved Dream a step away.

She laughed. "Don't even try it. No falling off for me today."

Jake blew a big, pink bubble. After it popped, he said, "The more I look at that mare, the more I think she's lost some weight. You'll be entered up in your first barrel race before you know it."

"Like you, she's been watching her diet, eating supplements, and jogging every afternoon."

"Good to know that your horse and I have something in common."

How could Jake always be so sure about things? He almost had her convinced. Miya pictured Dream, neck outstretched, running past the crowded stands. Miya leaned forward, urging her on. She could practically feel the wind blowing past and see the blurry ground beneath her. Miya heard the roar of the crowd. She heard the announcer say, "Miya Skippingbird's time is 17.22 seconds, putting her in the number one spot."

Jake's voice jolted her from her daydream. "What are you thinking about with that smile on your face?"

"Oh." Miya shook her head. She wasn't ready to share her daydream with anyone yet, not even Jake. She improvised. "I was just thinking how much I've missed you this year. In seventh grade, we had three classes together, plus lunch. Now I'm lucky to see you on the bus."

Jake took his rope down and swung it, successfully roping a sagebrush. "I know. Maybe we'll have better luck in high school."

"I hope so. We need to see each other more like when we were little."

Jake coiled his rope. "You're not kidding. Remember when we were six and you hit me in the head with the baseball bat?"

"That was an accident. I still feel bad about that. How about the time we were playing hide-and-go-seek? You went in and ate lunch and left me hiding under the horse trailer."

"I didn't know you would fall asleep under there."

Miya giggled. "And whose idea was it to give the kittens a bath in the horse trough?"

"Their paws were muddy."

Miya brushed a fly off Dream's neck. "Not to change the subject, but are you ready to ride next week?"

"Yeah. I'm looking forward to riding in some jackpots before the rodeo starts in June."

Miya nodded. "I saw the poster online. I'm gonna go watch you and stay for a while to watch the barrels." That way she could see how good the other girls were and decide if it would be too embarrassing for her to enter.

"Sweet." Jake crossed an irrigation ditch and turned Hawk toward the mountain. "Same plan as usual?"

Miya blew a pink bubble. "See you later."

While Jake and Cap went west, Miya headed east. After a few steps, she stopped and turned Dream so she could watch Jake for another minute. He rode with grace and confidence, leaning forward a little as Hawk climbed a hill. His hands were low and quiet, his heels down, his shoulders back and relaxed.

When Jake disappeared into a draw, Miya turned Dream toward the top of the mountain. She let Dream choose her own path around the fat green cacti with their sharp spines. In some places, they spread out like a gigantic carpet of tiny nails. Occasionally, they'd skirt a scrub juniper, its limbs twisted into a loose knot. Miya knew that was its response to the wind—wind that could be hot as a firecracker or cold as an afternoon of ice fishing.

Miya and Dream left the desert behind and began their climb to higher country. Sand and granite gave way to green meadows. Meadows dotted with wildflowers, red, purple, yellow, and white. It looked as though a giant had scattered handfuls of confetti across the field.

Dream swung her head around and pricked up her ears. Miya followed her gaze. At the edge of the meadow, a mama cow stood with her calf. Both mama and baby were shiny black.

"Good eyes, girl," Miya said, leaning forward and patting Dream's neck.

As they headed in that direction, the mama cow raised her head and stared at Miya. The baby trotted toward Dream. A brave step. Two. He was still several yards away from Miya when he turned and kicked up his little heels. The calf twisted and jumped and started back to his mama.

Miya laughed. "You sure are cute, little calf."

Moo. Moo.

The mama cow called to her calf and took a step toward Dream. Miya knew that the mama cow wanted to get between Miya and the calf to protect her baby.

The baby trotted over and disappeared behind the mama cow.

Miya started to ride around the pair. The mama cow watched Miya.

"Go on." Miya slapped her hand on her thigh. "Let's go."

Mama and baby started walking across the meadow. Miya and Dream followed. When she was sure they were headed toward the ranch, Miya turned Dream back.

Time to find another pair.

The sun rose higher in the sky, and Miya lifted her heavy hair off her neck and tied it back. She turned her face toward the breeze. Dream's neck developed a fine film of sweat. She still had a ways to go before she was in shape, but she worked hard.

Dream usually saw the pairs before Miya did. Some were in groups of four or six. One group of ten stood in the shade of a stand of cottonwood trees. Miya and Dream worked their way around them and got them headed toward the ranch. "Go on home, cows. Go on!" She'd wave her hand or slap her rope against her thigh. Mamas and fat, sleek babies ambled down the countryside toward the gate.

By midafternoon, they reached the end of the pasture and turned around. Jake would be pushing his group back, and the two parts of the herd would meet on the flat.

Miya heard Jake's group of cows before she saw them. When Jake saw Miya, he grinned and waved. "On to the gate."

Jake rode close to the front of the herd, keeping the cattle pointed in the right direction. Cap stayed close to Hawk. He watched and listened to Jake for the slightest hand signal or quiet word and jumped to obey.

Miya rode behind, keeping the cattle moving forward. Occasionally, a calf lost track of its mother and would turn and try to run back to the place he had last seen her. Miya would gather the reins and turn Dream toward the runaway calf. They would chase it, jumping over sagebrush, and return it to the herd.

Miya rode back and forth, back and forth, working hard to keep the herd bunched. Sweat ran down her back and arms, and hunger clawed at her belly. Worst of all, Dream stopped cooperating.

Hadn't Julia said Dream was good on cows? The mare shook her head and swished her tail. Dream had been super all morning. Miya wondered what the problem was now. Maybe she was tired? Grumpy? Miya tightened her reins. Again, Dream shook her head and swished her tail.

A calf started to turn back. Without waiting for Miya's signal, Dream sprang after it and brought the calf around. Miya loosened her reins. She put her hand down on Dream's mane. Without being guided, Dream walked back and forth behind the herd. She crowded the cows that were lagging and turned the calves back almost before Miya realized one had quit the herd.

Dream was trying to do her job, and Miya was getting in her way. Miya loosened her reins some more.

"Sorry, girl. I need to trust you more."

They arrived at the gate, and Miya kept the cattle bunched along the fence while Jake opened it wide. He jumped back on Hawk and stood a few feet back to count the pairs as they came through. Cap sat beside him, ears up.

Miya knew gates were tricky. She and Cap had to put enough pressure on the cows to encourage them to pass through the gate without scattering the herd. Today, it helped that the mama cows knew where they were going. It helped that Dream could read their minds and worked them quietly like a pro. Miya smiled. She couldn't wait to tell Dad he was right about Dream being smart.

After they got the last of the pairs through the gate, Miya and Jake dismounted, loosened the cinches, and got water and snacks out of the saddlebags.

"Dream's tired. She needs a break while the calves mother up," Miya said to Jake.

The cows and calves that had gotten separated on the way called to each other. Frantic moos echoed until the two met. When they did, the calves would stick their noses up under their mothers and nurse, bracing their legs and swishing their tails.

Jake knelt down and scratched Cap. Cap stretched out his neck and closed his eyes. "You're a good boy," Jake told him. Jake squirted his water bottle. A stream hit her in the middle of her back. "Hey!"

"Hey, yourself. What's wrong you?"

Miya looked at her saddle so she wouldn't have to look at Jake. "Why do you think something's bothering me?"

"Umm. Let me think. . . . Maybe because we've known each other forever."

Where could she start? Math class? Mean comments online? Barrel racing with Dream? Lily? Lily.

Miya felt her cheeks getting hot. "I've been a bad friend to Lily."

"How?"

Miya looked down at the bag of pretzels in her hand. "I kinda ditched her."

"How can you 'kinda ditch' somebody?" He opened a box of raisins.

Miya kicked at a rock on the ground and told Jake about Abigail and how mad Lily was at her and Lily's revenge. She almost told him about Lily's crush on him but stopped in time. She didn't want to talk about crushes.

When she finished, Jake watched the cows for a long time. They had settled down except for an occasional *MOO*. Finally, he shook his head.

"Girls. They're so dramatic."

"Is that all you have to say? I had hoped for some words of wisdom." She put the pretzels and water back into her saddlebags.

Jake tightened his cinch, put his foot in the stirrup, and stepped up in one smooth motion. He whistled for Cap. "Okay. Jake's words of wisdom. Talk to her in person. Don't hide behind your phone. Tell her you'll still hang out, just not at lunch." He shrugged. "She'll get over it."

Miya tightened her cinch and pulled herself into the saddle.

Boys.

Lily wouldn't just "get over it."

Chapter Fourteen

Sunday afternoon, Miya saddled Dream and rode down the lane to Abigail's house. Puffy clouds sailed across a light blue sky. A pickup rattled by with a cow dog pacing back and forth in the truck bed. He barked a sharp hello to Miya and Dream.

After Miya arrived at Abigail's house, she tied Dream to the hitching rail and unsaddled her. Abigail *TRIP-TRAPPED* down the path in her blue, plastic shoes. Two Hello-Kitty barrettes pinned back her hair. Miya winced at the barrettes. Didn't Abigail understand that kindergarten was the absolute cut off for Hello-Kitty anything?

"Hi. I saw you ride up. This must be Dream." She grasped both sides of Dream's halter and held her head still. She stared into Dream's eyes. Dream stared back.

"What are you doing?"

"I'm trying to see if your new horse has a kind eye," Abigail said. She continued to stare into Dream's eyes. Miya tried not to laugh.

"I think she does," Abigail said, straightening up. "But I don't usually go around looking into horses' eyes. Maybe Grandma can tell when she gets up from her nap. I promised her I wouldn't let you leave until she sees Dream."

Sprint and Foxy loped up to the fence with their heads and tails held high. They stopped at the gate and nickered to Dream. She nickered back and pawed at the ground.

Miya double-checked the half hitch to make sure the knot secure. "That's good because I hoped your grandma would take a look at her and maybe give me a few pointers. Let's get the math lesson over with first, and maybe she'll be up." Abigail opened the screen door and shut it quietly. They stepped into the kitchen to find the counters scrubbed and free of clutter. A fat, copper tea kettle sat on the stove as sunflower-print curtains flapped in the window. A single dirty glass sat in the sink.

Miya followed Abigail up the stairs to her room. Abigail's computer sat on a card table. Two frayed, green camping chairs were beside it.

While Abigail booted up the computer, Miya looked around. A one-eyed teddy bear rested on a faded pink quilt on the bed. A wooden dresser with a missing knob stood against one wall. Miya looked at the small mirror that hung above it. Not only was it small, but it was also cracked. How could Abigail see well enough to do her hair or check for zits?

The only picture in the room sat on the nightstand. Miya walked over and picked it up. A man and a woman in front of a river. The man held a toddler in his arms. Miya studied the picture a minute more. "Is this you?"

Abigail glanced at it, and her shoulders stiffened. She forced herself to look back at the computer. "That's my mom and dad right before they died."

Miya fumbled, nearly dropping the photo. "They're dead?" The room felt suddenly stuffy and hot, making it hard to breathe.

"Yeah. They were missionaries in Alaska. Flying small planes in the bush is crazy risky. They were on their way back from one of the villages when they crashed."

"Were you with them?"

"No, I was staying on the ranch in Montana with Grandma and Grandpa. Mom and Dad were on their last trip for a while. They were coming back to the lower forty-eight to help Grandma and Grandpa with the place."

"I'm . . . I'm . . . sorry." Miya couldn't imagine life without either Mom or Dad. But both? What if she didn't have a dad to tease her? To tell lame jokes and pretend to be offended when she rolled her eyes? Dad taught her how to drive a tractor, ride a horse, and work hard until the job was finished.

And Mom. Mom listened. She helped with school stuff, especially posters and presentations. Mom taught her to think about other people. She smelled like lavender lotion when she hugged Miya goodnight.

Miya looked at the picture again and back to Abigail.

"It's okay. Happened a long time ago." She crossed her arms and stared down at the card table.

Miya wanted to ask about the grandpa and the ranch and how they came to live in a broken-down farmhouse, but she stopped herself. Maybe she'd ask later when they were better friends.

Abigail turned the computer to face Miya. "Come on. Let's start with the first review question."

They worked steadily for an hour. Abigail started by working a problem, explaining each step. Miya wrote it all down in her math notebook and highlighted keywords in yellow. Sometimes she asked Abigail to repeat the steps two or three times. Abigail never got mad or looked down on Miya for not getting it right away. Abigail just explained it again, the second or third time more slowly. Then, Miya would try the same type of problem. At first, she got impatient and tried to skip a step or do it in her head, but Abigail stopped her.

"It's like a video game. Each step leads to the next level. If you solve all the levels, you solve the problem. If you skip steps or mess one up because you don't understand, you won't get to the next level." Abigail scrolled to the next set of problems. "Let's try some like these."

A little later, Miya shifted in the green camping chair. The plastic frame creaked. "You explain things so much better than Mr. Callahan. If we keep at this all week, I might be able to pass the test Thursday." An invisible weight lifted off her chest. Miya thought she might not be able to solve all the equations, but at least she'd be able to get partial credit on most of them.

"I know you'll pass, and then you can retake some of the earlier tests that you didn't do so well on." Abigail closed the computer. "Grandma should be up by now. Let's show her Dream."

Miya's eyes were drawn to the picture of Abigail's family. She clenched her teeth to bite back the tears. Miya didn't want to embarrass Abigail by acting like she felt sorry for her. Miya kept her head down while she followed Abigail out the door.

Lisa looked up as the girls clattered down the stairs. She smiled and pushed her crossword puzzle aside. "Hello, girls. Thanks for being so quiet while I napped. I'm rested and ready to go." Lisa reached for her cane. "I'm glad you rode your horse over, Miya. Shall we go take a look at her?"

"Grandma, Miya is getting up her courage to run Dream. She wants to know if you'll give her a few pointers."

Miya blushed. She wished Abigail hadn't blurted that out. She didn't want Lisa, a person who'd won the national finals, to think she had to "get up her courage," like some scaredy-cat preschooler.

Lisa pushed herself to her feet. "I'm happy to help if I can. There are few things in this world I enjoy better than watching a barrel horse."

Miya held the door open. Abigail switched off the kitchen lights. Lisa gripped the top of her cane, and the three made their way to the arena. When they arrived, Abigail ran to the barn and returned with the straight-backed wooden chair. Lisa settled down on it, leaning forward slightly, hands folded over her cane. Abigail sat cross-legged on the dirt beside her. The yellow cat appeared, and Abigail pulled her into her lap.

After saddling and bridling Dream, Miya led her inside the arena. As she pulled the gate shut, Miya noticed that a couple of the posts had rotted at the base. Three rusty metal barrels lined the east side of the arena.

Foxy and Sprint watched from the next field. They trotted back and forth along the fence, nickering and shaking their head.

Miya admired them for a minute, checked her cinch, and pulled herself into the saddle. "I'll trot and lope a few circles for you," she called.

Miya drew Dream's focus from Sprint and Foxy to her with a squeeze of her legs. Miya trotted and loped circles and figure eights. She stopped Dream and backed her up several steps.

Out of the corner of her eye, Miya saw Lisa nodding several times as Miya put Dream through her paces. "I like her," Lisa said half an hour later. "I think she's a good barrel prospect, and she'll make you a good friend."

Abigail transferred the yellow cat from her lap to the ground. She stood up and brushed the dirt off the seat of her pants. "I like your horse, too. Why don't you take her around the barrels, Miya? I'll help you set them up."

Miya ducked her head. "Should I?"

"If you're comfortable."

"How fast should I go?"

Lisa shrugged. "As fast as you want."

What is that supposed to mean?

Miya led Dream to the line of barrels. Miya grabbed the first one, careful not to cut her hands on the sharp rim. Should she trot and keep Dream under control? Should she lope? No one had ever won a barrel race by trotting or loping. Should she gallop? Lisa was used to seeing fast runs. Two monarch butterflies followed her as she set up the second barrel.

Miya watched Abigail roll the third barrel into place and turn it upright. Abigail wiped her hands on her thighs and ducked back through the rails. She jogged back toward her grandmother. Miya didn't want Lisa to think she was a fat scaredy-cat on a fat horse and decided to gallop.

At the gate, Miya turned Dream and lined her up with the first barrel. She gathered her reins, leaned forward in her saddle, picked the spot to run toward, and kicked. Dream, surprised, jumped into a lope. Miya kicked her again. Dream went faster.

Yes! They were galloping.

At the first barrel, Miya sat back in her saddle and pulled her right rein toward her belt buckle, asking Dream to turn. She'd misjudged her speed and waited too long to signal Dream, so they ran past the first barrel.

Miya groaned. She managed to turn Dream around the first barrel, but the rest of the run was choppy and off balance. Dream turned too soon at the second barrel and almost knocked it over. She swung wide on the third.

Miya felt the heat crawl up her neck and into her ears. It was bad enough to make a run like this in front of Abigail and Lisa, but what if it had happened in a competition? Everyone would laugh at her. The videos would be horrible. She stopped in front of the two and looked down at Dream's neck. "That was terrible."

Lisa smiled. "Don't beat yourself up about it. Everything breaks down with speed. Some good things happened. I can tell Dream understands the pattern and has a decent foundation. You have to review the basics again. Go back to a walk and trot and practice rating or slowing down at the right time for those turns."

Miya hesitated. Walk and trot? If she was ever going to get into a jackpot, she needed to practice going fast so she could compete with horses like Dragon.

As though reading her mind, Lisa continued. "Get all the steps perfected at a slow pace, and then the speed will come. If you don't turn your first barrel properly, it throws off the rest of your run. I'll write down some exercises you can work on at home."

"Thanks." Miya played with the rope strap on the front of her saddle. "That would be great."

"You're welcome. If you want to come over again after you've practiced, I'd be happy to give you a few more suggestions."

Miya stepped off Dream. She tied the mare up and walked back to the house behind Lisa and Abigail. The whole way Miya stared at the ground. As soon as she got through the door, Miya ran upstairs and got her math notebook. When Miya came down the stairs, Lisa sat at the kitchen table, drawing in a spiral notebook. She looked up and pointed to a chair beside her. "Come sit down for a minute, and I'll go over these diagrams with you."

The chair scraped across the linoleum as Miya pulled it out. She perched on the edge of the seat and stared at the penciled drawings as Lisa explained them. Arrows pointed to the path that Miya and Dream were supposed to follow as they worked on different drills. Lisa told her to set up cones and tires to practice turns without the barrels so Dream wouldn't get tired of going around the barrels. How could that work? Dream had to learn to run the barrels. Fast.

When Lisa finished, Miya nodded, folded the pages, and shoved them into her back pocket.

She said goodbye to both of them and ran back down to Dream. As she rode home, Miya looked over her shoulder. Abigail stood on the porch with her arm around her tiny grandma.

* * *

The next morning Miya waited at the bus stop. Wisps of white clouds chased each other across the sky. Miya watched them settle on top of the mountain. She pulled her hands up into her hoodie sleeves as she shifted from foot to foot. Miya wanted to fill Jake in on yesterday's ride before Abigail got on the bus.

After the bus arrived, Miya walked up the three steps and made her way down the aisle. She dropped into the seat beside Jake. He straightened and pulled out his earbuds. "Hey."

Miya pushed her backpack under the seat in front of her with her toe.

"Jake." Miya leaned toward him. "I've got a problem, and I need your advice before Abigail gets on the bus."

"Okay. What's up?"

Miya leaned closer. Her voice dropped to a half-whisper. "Yesterday, Dream and I made our first fast run. Abigail and her grandma watched. It was bad." She shook her head, remembering. "Real bad. Anyway, Lisa wrote down some exercises and offered to help me."

Jake raised his eyebrows. "That sounds good. What's the problem?"

Miya ran her hand through her hair. The scrunchie from her braid came out. "The problem is," she said but then paused. In a lower voice, she continued. "The problem is that Lisa is so old school. She won her buckle a hundred years ago. Barrel racers today do everything differently."

"Really?"

Miya glanced out the window. They'd pull up to Abigail's driveway soon. "Yes, really. Lisa has been so nice, and I don't want to sound mean, but if I do what she says, I'll never get past a lope. She wants me to go back to walking and trotting. I need help with going fast."

They pulled up to the bus stop. Miya could see Abigail out the window wearing a thin, pink windbreaker zipped up to her chin.

"Maybe you can do a little of both." Jake waved to Abigail. "If I were you, I'd start with the exercises Lisa gave you. Work hard on them. It's like having a trainer for free. You can still watch videos online and try some of that stuff, too."

Miya watched Abigail trip down the aisle in her blue, plastic shoes. Jake had it backward. She'd do a few of Lisa's exercises, but she'd focus on today's barrel winners. And today's winners went *fast*.

Chapter Fifteen

Miya walked toward her locker. The kids in the hall reminded her of avatars in a video game. They moved at high speed, bumping into each other and shooting off in all directions. Their hair, clothes, teeth, and gestures, all looked as though they were designed to be part of a middle-school video game.

Miya searched for Lily. She had a couple of minutes before math. She wished she'd never promised Jake that she'd talk to Lily, but she did. Now, she wanted to get it over with.

There.

Up ahead, Miya caught a glimpse of black hair with purple streaks.

Miya decided not to stop at her locker. She had what she needed for math. She hurried, pushing by clusters of students. "Lily, wait up."

Lily stopped outside Mr. Callahan's door. Lily crossed her arms over her tight, black tank top and tapped her foot until Miya caught up. Miya could see her bra. Lily should have worn a black bra if she was going to show so much of it. Beige looked funny.

"What?" Lily spat out the word like a challenge.

"Here's the whole truth this time." Miya took a deep breath. "I didn't mean to ditch you. But after Abigail got bullied in the cafeteria, I couldn't stand to see it happen again. So I tried to help by hiding her in the art room."

Lily rolled her eyes. "I didn't bully her. Mitchell did. All I did was video like everyone else."

"No, it wasn't just Mitchell. It was all of us. Anyone who didn't stand up to help, me included."

Lily twisted her mouth into a sneer. "Saint Miya, admit it. You ditched me because you don't care about me anymore."

"That's not true. Lily, I . . ."

But Lily overrode her. "Whatever. It's fine. Just tell me when Jake is riding."

Miya took another deep breath. She didn't want her voice to shake. "You really hurt me when you posted that picture of Moose Miya."

"Good. Now you understand how it feels."

Miya wanted to argue and make Lily understand how awful she felt, but the words stuck in her throat. "The series starts Saturday. 9:00 a.m. Silver Spur Arena."

Lily stared at her. "I'll be there, but I still hate you, Mega Miya." She stomped down the hall, her jeans tight and low.

Mr. Callahan appeared at his door. He didn't speak as he polished his thick, black-framed glasses with a handkerchief. Miya wondered how much he had heard. As the bell rang, she slipped inside the room and sat at her desk. Mr. Callahan set his glasses on the top of his head. His polyester pants *SWISH-SWISHED* as he strode down the aisle to the front of the classroom. Miya opened her computer.

She tried to push thoughts of Lily out of her mind and pay attention to the lesson. As usual, Mr. Callahan covered the whiteboard with numbers and letters. Today, she kind of understood it. Most of it, in fact. She had a couple of questions but didn't dare raise her hand. She'd ask Abigail later.

At lunch, Miya hurried to the yellow wing. She pushed open the heavy door of the art room. It smelled of paint thinner and paper and something else. . . . Did creativity have a smell? As she unpacked the egg salad sandwiches, Miya looked around. A gangly boy with bony wrists stooped over the sink, rinsing paintbrushes. A girl shoved some sort of tool into a block. Mr. O checked through portfolios, one brown cowboy boot tapping in time to the country music.

Miya carefully pulled her armature out of the closet by its base. She found a box of beige, polymer clay. Miya walked to her favorite table, the one farthest away from the speakers blaring country music.

Miya powered up her laptop and loaded her favorite video on how to sculpt a horse. She'd watched it a hundred times, but it felt reassuring to have a real sculptor at her elbow. She glanced at the bottom right-hand corner of her computer. Abigail was late, so Miya decided to get started on her sculpture. Abigail usually reviewed the day's math lesson while they ate, but since Abigail wasn't here yet, math would have to wait.

Miya opened the package of clay, held it up to her nose, and sniffed. Closing her eyes, she smiled. The smell reminded her of the mud pies she used to make with Lily when they were little. Miya pushed Lily out of her mind. She didn't want thoughts of Lily to ruin this project for her.

The clay felt smooth and cool. Miya rubbed her fingertips gently over it and pictured her sculpture. For the first time, she didn't imagine any race horse—she pictured Dream.

Carefully, Miya wrapped the strips of clay around the armature. She started in the middle and worked toward the back. She took her time, making sure to overlap the strips and blend them with her fingers. Wrapping and smoothing. The video said to push all the air out between the aluminum foil and the clay. That was fine with her. Pressing and smoothing also helped reduce bulk. This wasn't going to be a massive draft horse, but a graceful running horse. This was going to be Dream.

Abigail rushed in. "Sorry, I'm late. I was talking to some kids about math club. They're meeting all summer so they'll be ready for the math team in high school."

Miya looked up. "It's fine. I need to get this first layer on so Mr. O can bake it. Wait . . . Math all summer? Ugh. Shoot me now."

"Math for me is like art for you." Abigail helped herself to a sandwich and wandered over to talk to Isabel.

* * *

Miya stepped off the bus and walked down the lane toward her house. Lilac bushes pushed against the fence. Bees buzzed among the fat purple blossoms. She'd been stung lots of times trying to pick flowers for Mom. Giving the bees a wide berth, she continued on. Miya sat down on the tire swing, its black rubber warm against her legs. Idly, she pushed against the ground with her toes. She hadn't swung in years. The rope was stiff and frayed now. Weeds grew underneath.

When she was little, she would climb on the swing, and Dad would wind the rope until the old limb that held it squeaked and moaned. Miya would lean all the way back, gripping the rough edge of the tire with both hands. Her dad would count, "One, two, three . . ." and let go.

Around and around she twirled as the rope unfurled. The stars flew by in great sweeping circles. They looked like millions of polka dots dancing in the sky.

WHOOSH. WHOOSH.

When the swing finally stopped, Dad would scoop her up and hold her until the dizziness passed, and then she'd beg to do it again.

Her life felt like that now. One, two, three, and the rope unfurled. Only, unlike a ride on a tire swing, Miya didn't want her life to spin around and around. Events in her life flew by with such dizzying speed that Miya couldn't control it.

Zoey trotted down the driveway, speeding up when she saw Miya. Her bright green tennis ball dropped at Miya's feet. Zoey's ears stood up as she looked from the ball to Miya and back again. Miya jumped off the swing, grabbed the ball, and threw it as hard as she could toward the house. Zoey bounded after it.

Dream nickered from the corral. "Be right back," Miya called to her. "I have to change my clothes." Miya abandoned the swing and finished her walk to the house. She opened the door and stopped in the kitchen. Miya had been so busy working on the sculpture that she'd skipped lunch. Now, she was starving. Miya opened cupboard after cupboard. Walnuts and almonds. No cookies? No candy? No chips? Miya settled for a box of raisins.

Zoey looked up at her with hope. "You don't like raisins, remember? I'll ask Mom to step it up. More junk food for me. More dog treats for you."

Miya climbed the stairs to her bedroom with Zoey trailing behind. She reached into her back pocket and pulled out some crumpled pieces of paper—the exercises Lisa had drawn for her. Miya smoothed out one of the pages and studied it.

1. *MAKE A 30-FOOT CIRCLE OUT OF TIRES.*
2. *REMOVE ONE TIRE AND SUBSTITUTE A BARREL.*
3. *RIDE WITH BOTH HANDS AND USE YOUR HANDS AND LEGS TO KEEP DREAM IN THE PROPER ARC AS YOU WALK AROUND THE CIRCLE.*
4. *OCCASIONALLY, TURN THE BARREL WHEN YOU GET TO IT.*
5. *RESUME WALKING.*

MIYA'S DREAM

DO THIS IN BOTH DIRECTIONS. FIRST AT A WALK.
THEN A TROT.

Several more exercises followed. All involved walking, trotting, backing, and something called "counter-arcing," whatever that was.

Miya dropped the pages back on her dresser. She would try one exercise as a warm-up, but she wasn't spending too much time on it. Dream had to be ready to run. Miya changed to knee socks and pulled on her boots.

She walked out to the corral and haltered Dream. She offered her an alfalfa cube and laughed as the mare's whiskers tickled her palm.

Miya tied Dream up and stepped back, looking at her. She had rolled quite a few times since Miya had brushed her, and now she looked as ratty as the stuffed bunny Miya used to carry around when she was two. Dream's winter coat shed in clumps, and mud caked her neck and hind legs. Little pieces of brown sagebrush snarled in her tail.

"I see you've been enjoying yourself while I've been slaving away at school." Miya retrieved the grooming kit from the tack room and selected a shedding blade, a long flexible piece of metal with small teeth on one side. She pulled the teeth across Dream's body, starting at her neck, but not on Dream's head or lower legs where the bones were close to the surface. The teeth grasped the loose hair and pulled it out. Soon, the ground was covered with black and white hair. With a gust of wind, the hair floated in the air like dandelion fuzz, coating Miya's lips and stealing its way into her mouth.

"Yuck." She coughed and tried to spit it out.

Miya finished grooming Dream and saddled her. Miya grabbed a tire from the stack behind the machine shed. She

121

rolled it down to the arena and flopped it down. She wiped her hands across the front of her jeans and went back three more times to get more tires. After arranging the tires in a circle on the east end of the arena, Miya rolled an extra barrel over and set it in the circle of tires. Finally, she was ready to ride.

Miya bridled Dream and led her into the arena. She tightened the cinch, pulled up her jeans, and struggled to get up on her horse. Miya picked up her reins and looked longingly at the barrels set up in a cloverleaf pattern in the west end of the arena. Since it had taken her so long to get ready today, maybe she should run through the barrel pattern a couple of times and start with the exercise tomorrow. To make up for missing today, she could do two of the exercises on Lisa's list.

To warm up, Miya walked, trotted, and loped a few circles. As she rode, Miya thought about all the things she had to do that evening. Miya had homework and chores. She needed to wash her hair, and, of course, she needed to watch more barrel-racing videos. She'd run barrels today and do Lisa's exercises tomorrow.

"Dream, I promise we'll work on foundation skills tomorrow." Miya pictured Lisa frowning at her and felt guilty.

Miya rode to the west end of the arena. She turned and faced the first barrel in the cloverleaf pattern. Miya ran Dream straight toward the barrel. As Dream started into the turn, she hit the barrel with her shoulder and knocked it over.

Darn. Miya looked down at the blue, plastic barrel lying on its side. Dream's footprints in the sand showed that she rode too close to the barrel. Miya got down and set up the barrel. Disgusted with herself, she kicked the sand and then smoothed it out with her boot. If Dream and Miya tipped over a barrel in a race, they would receive a five-second penalty. A five-second penalty would lose the race.

Now that Dream had a taste of speed, she wanted to run. She jogged behind Miya as Miya led her back to the gate. Dream shook her head and snorted. When Miya tried to get up on her, Dream danced away. Miya tightened her left rein, but each time she got her foot close to the stirrup, Dream spun in a circle around her.

Miya huffed in frustration. "Dream, if you would let me get on, we'll run again." Miya managed to grab the saddle horn, and after hopping around beside Dream, got her leg up over the back of the saddle.

Miya faced the first barrel again. Dream knew that she would soon be running toward it. She shook her head as Miya tightened her reins. "Whoa, girl."

Miya held her reins in her left hand and patted Dream's neck with her right hand. Dream's muscles bunched as hard as river rock under Miya's fingertips. To settle her horse down, Miya walked Dream in a small circle. When Miya was ready, she loosened the reins. Dream surged forward. This time they managed to get around all three barrels without knocking any of them over. The run was choppy, but at least all three barrels were upright when Miya and Dream got back to the gate.

Miya knew Lisa would tell her to quit there for the afternoon. Miya should stop on a positive note, but she knew the next run would be even faster. "Let's do it, just one more time," Miya said to Dream.

Dream ran to the first barrel, her neck stretched out, ears back. As she turned it, she knocked it over. Dream hesitated, but Miya leaned forward asking Dream to keep running. She and Dream would do a better job with the next two barrels.

Miya couldn't believe it when Dream knocked over the second barrel, too. They managed to leave the third barrel standing.

When Miya got back to the gate, she got off Dream and winced as she stared at the two barrels resting on their sides.

"That was a terrible run, girl, but don't worry. I'm watching a bunch of videos tonight."

* * *

Miya slumped in her chair and stared at the bulletin board in the art room. Layers of paper sprinkled with thumbtacks covered every inch. Like her thoughts, it was a jumbled mess. She stared down at the disarray of her sculpture. She hadn't imagined it would be this hard, especially when the artists online made it look so simple. Their expert hands built up the clay and shaved it away, smoothed it, and refined it. As if by magic, a muscle would appear, or a joint, or a feathery mane.

Miya had no magic in her hands. Yesterday, she'd struggled the whole period trying to get the knee joints and the muscles in the shoulders right. She left without being satisfied.

Now, Abigail worked on a pencil sketch at the other end of the table. Her small shoulders hunched. "Miya," said Abigail looking up and setting down her pencil, "is there anything I can do to help you? I could search for another video or get you a drink or . . ." Abigail's voice trailed off.

Miya shook her head. "I don't think there's anything you can do, but thanks."

She stared at the armature. How much clay to add? How much to take off? Which tool was best for lines? Which tool was best for blending? Tears of frustration welled up behind her eyes and threatened to spill over. She looked up to see Mr. O ambling toward her. Miya looked down again.

Oh, no. Not Mr. O.

He'd warned her. Now, he might insist she give up on the running horse and make a stupid horse head.

Even though Miya and Dream were having a tough time in the practice pen, Miya knew she had to keep trying to make a running horse. She couldn't settle for less. Miya wished she could capture the spirit of happiness and freedom that welled up inside her when she was galloping a fast horse—the ground whooshing by underneath her, the air skimming past her, her laughter dancing and twirling like butterflies in the high country.

"So, Miya," Mr. O said as he perched on the stool next to her and hooked the heel of his cowboy boot over a rung. "Let's see what you have here." Wordlessly, she shoved the sculpture at him. He considered it for a minute.

Humming to himself, Mr. O built a small horse figure out of clay, the kind she'd made in third grade. He picked up one of the wooden tools with a pointed end. He explained how to use it to create lines for muscles as his fingers moved over the clay. He smoothed it out. "You try." Miya picked up the pointed tool and the small statue. She closed her eyes for a second. Miya pictured Mr. O's hands as he made the lines.

She opened her eyes and tried to copy the way he held the tool, the amount of pressure he used, and the angle he held the statue. Miya's line wiggled down the statue's neck. She smoothed it out. She tried again. Each time, the muscle looked a little more realistic.

Mr. O shoved his stool back. "We'll work on a tool a day until we get the most important ones covered."

Miya looked up at him and back down at the little horse statue in her hand. She didn't want Mr. O to see how disappointed she was. On the one hand, Miya felt relieved that he would help her make a running horse, but on the other, this project would take forever! At this rate, she'd never get her sculpture done. What choice did she have? Miya nodded. Not trusting herself to speak.

"Don't get discouraged, Miya. Sculpting takes practice, just like riding a barrel horse."

Mr. O started to move toward Tess who worked on a torn paper collage.

He looked at Abigail's sketch on his way. "Umm. Good grass," he said.

"Thanks." Abigail beamed.

Miya watched him walk away. Mr. O was right. If she wanted to be happy with the way Dream turned out, she couldn't take shortcuts.

* * *

Miya skidded into the empty locker room. All the other kids were already outside running warm-up laps. Miya twirled the combination on her locker. She threw open the door as her clothes tumbled out. Miya scooped them off the floor and quickly changed before jogging out onto the field. The class stood next to the coach while the team captains assigned positions.

Coach looked up from her clipboard and frowned. "Miya, you've been late every day this week. I've had it. I'm counting you tardy."

"Sorry." Miya bent down to tie her shoes. She'd been in too much of a hurry to do it in the locker room. "I was working on a project in the art room, and time got away from me."

"Doesn't cut it, young lady. Exercise is important for everyone but especially for . . . ." Coach stopped midsentence.

MIYA'S DREAM

A ripple of laughter spread through the class as a couple of kids puffed out their cheeks and pretended to stretch their T-shirts over huge stomachs. Miya knew that the kids had mentally filled in the rest of the coach's sentence with *for you heavy kids.*

Embarrassed and flushed, she crouched over her shoes.

Don't cry. Don't cry.

The coach cleared her throat. "We've wasted enough time. Miya, you're on the blue team. Everyone out on the field. Hustle! Hustle!"

Fighting tears, Miya didn't move. She heard soft footfalls. Small neon-green shoes appeared. Someone crouched down and a light arm wrapped around her shoulders.

Miya chanced a look at the girl.

"Hey, Miya," Emily, the fixer girl from math, whispered. "Don't let the old bat get you down. Her hemorrhoids are probably acting up again."

Miya felt a smile tug at the corners of her mouth. She sniffed. "Someone should give her some Preparation H."

Emily grabbed Miya's hand and pulled her to her feet. "You got that right. Come on, you're on my team today." Emily flipped her French braid over her shoulder and pushed back her headband. Together, she and Miya jogged out onto the soccer field.

Chapter Sixteen

Miya and Abigail sat together on the bus, Miya's math notebook open in front of them. The Dream sculpture was taking all of Miya's lunchtime, so they used the bus ride for math tutoring. Abigail and Miya started their second problem when Miya felt a slight jolt as the driver put the bus into gear. Miya looked up. Lily stepped on the bus and marched straight down the aisle, her brother in tow. Lily stopped when she reached Jake's seat. Lily pointed to the seat in front of Jake, and Noah sat down. Without asking, Lily plopped down next to Jake. As she slid her purple backpack under the seat in front of her, she shot Miya a challenging glare.

Jake opened his eyes, straightened in his seat, and pulled out his earbuds. "Hey, Lily." He leaned forward. "Hey, Noah."

"Hi, Jake."

Lily scooted in close to him. Jake moved closer to the window. Lily scooted over again, even closer. Jake glanced across at Miya in the seat across the aisle and raised his eyebrows. Miya shrugged in reply.

Jake cleared his throat. "So, uh, you guys are riding the bus today."

"Yeah." Lily nibbled on her fingernail. "Mom's having car trouble. Again. She's getting a ride from a lady at work until she can get the car fixed." Lily turned her bracelet around and around on her wrist. "Looks like we'll be riding the bus with you for a while."

"Oh, that's cool. I mean, not about your mom's car trouble, but about you guys riding the bus some."

Miya glanced over. Jake looked uncomfortable crammed in the seat corner against the window.

Lily looked at Miya and Abigail, her eyes cold. She turned back to Jake. "I'm glad you're still my friend, unlike some people I know."

Abigail leaned across the aisle. "Hey . . ." Miya put her hand on Abigail's shoulder and shook her head. Lily wasn't ready to listen.

Lily whipped around in her seat to face Abigail. "What?"

"Nothing," said Miya.

Abigail searched Lily's face. "Nothing."

"Good." Lily faced Jake again. "Like I was saying, I hear you're gonna ride this weekend."

Jake nodded. "I'm entered up in the series that starts this Saturday."

Lily twirled her bracelet some more. "Dad's gonna drop me off so I can watch you ride. I'll have to bring the little kids with me cuz Mom's working."

"That's cool," Jake said.

Miya forced herself to concentrate on the next math problem, but Lily laughed and brushed Jake's arm. Miya chewed on the pencil's eraser. She knew Jake was nice to everybody, but it sounded like he was having fun with Lily. Miya wished she were sitting beside him instead of trying to figure out this dumb math assignment.

* * *

A horsefly landed on Dream's neck, and Miya smacked it. *Crunch.* She took her hand away and saw a glob of blood on Dream's neck. Miya turned her hand over and saw blood there, too.

Yuck.

Miya wiped it on her thigh. As soon as she killed one, others took their place.

129

Geez!

Although she'd sprayed Dream with bug spray before she got on, horseflies and black flies tormented them both. Miya frowned at the tire that Dream was circling at a walk. She tried to work on Lisa's exercises, at least a few of them. One of the problems of going so slow was it gave the flies plenty of time to harass them.

Miya slapped at another fly and missed. She huffed in frustration. These drills were really boring. Miya changed directions and walked around the tire the other way. If they went any slower, Miya would die of boredom, and the vultures would be circling instead of the flies.

Miya nudged Dream into a trot. As they rode through a cloud of tiny black gnats, Miya waved her hand in front of her face. She zigzagged across to the second tire on the other side of the arena. She rode back across to the third. Back and forth they trotted until they had circled all six. Miya tried to pay attention to the placement of her hands, legs, feet, and weight. All of it overwhelmed her brain. She rode the zigzag pattern twice more and set up the barrels. She ran them three times.

Lisa's exercises didn't seem to be helping. All three times she overshot the first barrel, so the other turns were awkward and slow. Fortunately, no flies caught up with them.

Dad walked through the barn and out to the arena. He leaned on the fence. "How is Dream doing?"

She trotted over. "We're having problems with the first barrel. Let me show you."

Miya trotted over to the gate. She leaned forward and asked Dream to run toward the barrel. Miya used both hands to help guide Dream. They made it around the barrel—barely. Miya ran the rest of the pattern and stopped by Dad.

Dad ducked through the rails and took ahold of Dream's bridle. "Calm down, girl," he said. He rubbed Dream's neck. She lowered her head and stood quietly.

Dad looked at Miya. "Dream is definitely shouldering the first barrel. If I were you, I'd slow things down to a walk and trot to reteach Dream how to turn it. Did Lisa give you some exercises for that?"

"Yes." Miya swatted at a horsefly. "But I'm watching videos online. I like getting advice from real barrel horse trainers."

"Cool her down, feed her, and come eat supper. Tomorrow's a new day."

Chapter Seventeen

Miya, Mom and Dad, and Janelle sat in the stands closest to the bucking chutes. The white paint of the wooden planks peeled off in flakes. Janelle chewed her lower lip. Looking down from the stands, Miya could see Jake's dad and uncle talking to the other dads by the bucking chutes. Most of them wore a championship buckle from a long-ago rodeo.

Mom pointed to the next set of bleachers. "Isn't that Lily and her brother and sister? You should invite them to sit with us."

Miya turned and saw Lily perched on the bottom row of the bleachers. Her purple tank top matched the streaks in her hair. She scrolled through her phone while Noah and Paislee climbed around on the bleachers behind her.

Last summer when things were okay between Lily and her, Lily and her brother and sister had watched lots of rodeos with Miya's family. Miya wished that things were still okay between them. Miya closed her eyes. What if things never went back to the way they were supposed to be?

Miya sighed and turned to Mom. "I don't think she wants to. She's been mad at me lately."

Mom arched her eyebrows but let it go.

One of the clowns wandered by. He had big white circles painted around his eyes, and bright red makeup covered his nose. The clown led a black and white border collie pup by a strand of orange baling twine. In the arena, blaring country music competed with the slow *CHUG-CHUG* of the tractor. Dragging a disc, it circled the arena, turning up the dirt to make it softer.

The miniature bulls bellowed as they made their way up the alley and into the chutes. Little kids in cowboy boots stood on the pipe fence outside the alley and stepped off like dominoes.

They hopped back up as soon as the bulls passed and scrambled to the top rail to claim the best seats in the house.

Miya glanced around the stands. On rodeo nights, they were mostly full of people eating popcorn and cotton candy. She could always tell which fans had never been to a rodeo before. They sat up straight. New boots. Cheap, brand-new cowboy hats. Miya smiled. Most of the time they had their hats on backward, an unmistakable sign of a true dude.

But today's event was a jackpot, and Miya liked jackpots— less pressure than a rodeo. Mini bull riding and barrel racing were the only two things on the program. The top three contestants won a percentage of the entry fees and points toward a season-end buckle.

The first bull riders climbed onto the catwalks behind the chutes. Miya's eyes lingered on Jake. Bull rope draped over one arm. Helmet tucked under the other. Miya knew Jake probably wore his lucky socks today, even though one of them had a hole in the heel.

Puffing clouds of black exhaust, the tractor chugged out the gate. The loudspeakers crackled. "Please stand for the national anthem." Two barrel racers dashed into the arena. The flags they carried snapped in the wind. One girl rode a palomino with a flaxen mane and tail. The other girl rode a tall black Thoroughbred who shook his head, fighting the bit. His rider's hands held him in check. The Thoroughbred wanted to run. They circled the arena at a gallop while the national anthem played.

Miya's heart *THUMP-THUMP-THUMPED* against her chest as she watched the girls race around the arena. She could never compete with horses like those, not unless Dream got faster. Much faster.

After the barrel racers left, groups of two spread out into the arena ready to do their jobs: two judges with clipboards and stopwatches; two men to pull the chute gate open when the rider nodded; two clowns in baggy shorts, suspenders, and running shoes; two pickup men on stout horses, shaking down their ropes; and two EMTs by the ambulance parked just outside the gate.

With pickup men to rope any bull that got too ornery and EMTs standing by, Jake would be fine if something went wrong.

Yep, Jake would be fine.

Miya's stomach felt like grasshoppers jumping around inside it. She jiggled her right foot up and down. At least she wouldn't have to wait for hours. Jake was one of the first riders up. After Jake had dropped down into the chute and sat on his bull, his dad leaned over and pulled the bull rope snug. Jake's uncle had his arm across the front of Jake's chest. He'd help Jake out if the bull acted up in the chute.

CLANG.

Chute number one opened. A contestant in lime-green chaps burst into the arena. The white bull he rode flung his head, spraying snot. The bull jumped and twisted each time he hit the ground. After a few seconds, Miya glimpsed a flash of daylight between the bull's back and the boy's rear end. In the next instant, he was on the ground. The clowns darted in. One jumped between the bull and the boy while the other turned the bull toward the gate. The boy stood up, dusted off his green chaps, and picked up his rope.

"3.8 seconds," the announcer blared. "Ladies and gentlemen, a qualified ride is 8 seconds, so all he takes home is your applause. No time for that cowboy."

Jake's mom straightened and pointed her phone toward the chutes. All Miya could see was the top of Jake's dad's hat as he leaned over the chute. Miya felt too nervous to do anything but watch. The first one ready would be the next one to ride, and it was . . . Jake!

The gate swung open. A brown and white spotted bull leaped out. After the first hard jump, Jake was still balanced perfectly over his rope, his free hand in the air. The long red fringe on his chaps snapped back and forth with each buck.

"Go, Jakie, go!" yelled Jake's mom.

"Go, Jake, go!" echoed Mom.

Miya stomped her feet on the bleachers. "Yeah, Jake!"

In the next instant, the bull changed his strategy. Instead of bucking away from the chutes, he began to spin in a circle. As though in slow motion, Jake slid to the side of the bull. He hung on for another long moment as the bull continued to spin.

THUD.

Jake hit the ground and didn't move as the bull bucked away. The mothers froze. Miya inhaled a sharp breath and clenched her fists. She focused on the still body lying in the arena dirt.

"Come on, Jake," she whispered. "Get up."

The gate *CLANG-CLANG-CLANGED* as the EMTs pushed through. Jake rolled over on to his hands and knees and struggled to his feet. He stood for a minute, bracing himself. He had a short conversation with a heavy woman in a blue uniform. Jake straightened up, pulled off his helmet, accepted his bull rope from the clown, and looked up to where his mom sat in the stands. He gave her a short wave. He was okay.

The crowd exhaled a collective sigh of relief. "5.1 seconds for Jake Runningdeer," the announcer said.

Miya slumped back on the bleachers. Jake was okay. That was the important thing. On the other hand, Miya thought he was disappointed. He made no day money and hadn't received any points toward the series buckle. Nothing. Nothing but applause.

Jake's dad and uncle climbed up into the stands.

Jake's mom scooted over. "Is he really okay?" Worry sharpened her voice, like sleet hitting the window.

After sitting beside his wife, Jake's dad put an arm around her shoulders. "Yes, Janelle. He's fine. Just had the wind knocked out of him is all. He'll be back to riding in no time. He's tough."

Jake's mom sagged against him. "Did you make Jake go to the EMT tent, or did you just take his word for it?"

"Now, honey, you know me better than that. I was standing right there when the EMTs gave him a clean bill of health. Isn't that right, Jimmie?" Jake's dad looked to his brother for support.

"Yep, Janelle. He's fine. He'll be here in a minute. You know how particular he is about stowing his gear in his riggin' bag."

Jake's mom looked unconvinced.

"You don't need to take our word for it." Jimmie pushed his hat back and grinned. "Here comes our future world champion now."

Riggin' bag slung over his shoulder, Jake wove his way through the crowd toward them.

As Jake approached, Lily stepped out, forcing him to stop. He high-fived Paislee and fist-bumped Noah. Lily rested her hand on Jake's arm and tossed her hair. Miya shook her head. How obvious could Lily get? Jake and Lily talked for a minute, and then he turned and pointed to Miya and his family in the stands. Lily shook her head. Jake shrugged. After one more fist bump for each of the little ones, he turned and climbed the rest of the way toward the group. Miya smiled. Jake had no visible bruises, and he sure looked good in his blue jeans and boots.

When he reached them, Jake dropped his riggin' bag and gave his mom a one-armed hug, and the guys slapped him on the back. Miya looked at her hands as she searched for the right words to cheer up her friend. But the crazy thing was Jake didn't seem disappointed. A grin split his face, not a half-hearted kind of grin, but a genuine I-just-won-a-big-victory kind of grin.

"I can't wait to ride next time. I know I was a little behind when he started to spin, so my bull . . ." He launched into a discussion with his dad and uncle.

Miya shook her head. Jake could have been hurt. Big time. Plus, he lost. And now, he laughed, talked, and planned for next time. Miya heard snatches of conversation about how they'd get Jake on more practice calves, how he'd work on not getting his feet behind him, how he'd use his free hand better.

Twenty-two riders later, the bull riding ended. The winners were announced. The tractor chugged back out to work up the ground for the barrel racing.

Jake slid down to the bleachers next to Miya. He hit her lightly on the arm. "Hey, let's go get some nachos before they start chasin' tin cans."

Miya hit him back.

"Ouch!" he said as he laughed. He was still pumped, excited, and confident he'd do better when he rode again.

"Aren't you disappointed you didn't make it to the whistle?"

Jake took off his cowboy hat and studied the wild turkey feather in the hat band. "I would have liked to win, but today's ride was one of the best I've ever made, so my training is paying off. Next time, I won't make the same mistakes and might even make the buzzer."

Miya wished she had the confidence Jake had. She wished she could look at the world like Jake did. But reality was reality. He was Jake Runningdeer, and she was Mega Miya.

"Nachos sound good, but Dream and I are both watching our weight. No extra cheese for me."

After waiting in line at the concession stand for nearly twenty minutes, Miya and Jake settled down on the bleachers with their nachos in their laps. Jake sat on one side of her, Dad on the other. They made it back just in time to see the first barrel racer enter the arena.

Miya looked over at Dad and smiled. "Do you want a nacho?"

He smiled back and shook his head as an Appaloosa horse trotted down the alley into the arena. He was white—black spots the size of tennis balls dotted his body. A short rattail wrung around and around in a circle the whole time he ran. He and his rider had a respectable time of 18.76. Miya thought he didn't run as hard as he could between the barrels. One day Dream might be able to beat him. If Miya ever got up the nerve to race, of course.

Next, the black horse whose rider carried the flag that morning charged down the alley toward the arena. His rider, a thin girl in a white cowboy hat, stood up in her stirrups to control him. At the last minute, she loosened her hands, and he dashed toward the first barrel. He ran flat out and low to the ground as though a wolf chased him. The black horse knocked over the first barrel and then the second. He somehow missed the third. With two five-second penalties, his time was 30.05.

Ouch.

"See," Dad whispered. "That's what happens when you have all speed and no control."

Miya nodded. "I feel bad for that girl."

The palomino, the other horse who had carried the flag, loped down the alley. When he hit the arena, he shifted into high gear. Each turn was perfect. His long strides ate up the ground between the barrels. As he ran home, his mane and tail streamed out behind him in a streak of liquid gold. His time: 18.00.

"Wow," Miya whispered to Jake. "If only I had a horse like that, and if only I could ride like that, my life would be perfect."

Jake snorted. "Don't be blinded by the bling. You do have a horse like that if you'd start believing in her. You can ride like that if you'd start believing in yourself."

"But, Jake, . . ."

Jake cut her off. "I'm tired of listening to excuses. Decide you're gonna do it. You may not win the first time out. Heck, you might not win the next twenty times, but you'll be a whole lot faster than you are sitting in the stands daydreaming about it."

Miya stared at him, stung. Not a hint of a smile on his face. That wasn't like Jake. He should be laughing, teasing, joking, and not staring at her with serious brown eyes.

Dad climbed to his feet. He looked at Miya and Jake. "That's good advice you just gave Miya, Jake. You should think about it, Miya." He turned to the group. "Is everyone ready to head home?"

Miya stomped down the bleachers ahead of the group. Easy for Jake to say. No one called him fat. No one posted horrible comments about him online.

Miya stared down at the cement as they walked by the concession stand. What if it were a matter of making a leap and getting the first race over with? Afterward, she could concentrate on improving her time. Dream was fast, and they were getting around the barrels better. If she lost her nerve before the actual race, she could always scratch.

Both families strolled along, reliving Jake's ride. When Miya passed the office, she stopped and stared at the little wood building with the sagging door. A fat bee buzzed at the top, trying to get in.

She'd show Jake she wasn't just a dreamer.

"Hey, Miya! Where are you going?"

Miya ignored him and dug into her pocket for the entry fee. Before she could back out, she opened the door and followed the bee inside. She stepped up to the counter and signed up for next Saturday's race.

* * *

Monday morning, the bus bumped over the potholes in the uneven pavement. Lily sat half-turned in the seat in front of Jake and Miya. Abigail sat across the aisle from Miya with her nose buried in a book.

While Miya sat beside Jake, his brown eyes smiled at her from under his Wyoming Cowboys ballcap.

"I can't believe you just walked in and signed up." He shook his head in admiration.

Miya frowned. "It's all your fault. You with your talk about 'no more excuses and daydreams.'" Lily turned completely around in her seat. "Signed up for what?"

"Miya's gonna run barrels next Saturday." Jake grinned, unable to contain how proud of her he was. Miya blushed and smiled back.

Lily's gaze settled on Miya. "Really? Hmm." Lily ran her eyes up and down Miya. "Are you sure that's a good idea? From your posts online, it looks like your horse is kind of heavy, and you, well uh, aren't you the plus-size version of most of those girls?"

Miya sat back, hurt.

"Wait a minute, Lily. Miya's been working really hard. Don't be mean."

Before Lily could reply, Abigail looked up from her book. She pushed her glasses up on her nose and glared at Lily. "I agree with Jake. Miya and Dream will do just fine. You'll see."

"Oh, I plan to see. In fact, I wouldn't miss it for the world." Lily smirked and turned around.

Chapter Eighteen

Miya began the long trek down the empty hallway. Since all the kids were in their classrooms, it was quiet, so quiet that Miya ended up tiptoeing the last few feet to her math classroom. It felt wrong to break the silence.

Miya saw Mr. Callahan's hunched back through the open door. He slurped soup as he stared at the screen. Miya thought that Mr. Callahan slurped louder than Zoey when she lapped up the left-over French toast batter on Saturday mornings.

"Mr. Callahan?"

He seemed absorbed in whatever was on the screen. Miya started down the aisle toward him. She raised her voice a bit.

"Umm, Mr. Callahan?"

Mr. Callahan whipped around in his chair so fast his spoon clattered to the floor. Miya glanced at his screen. Solitaire.

"What are you doing sneaking around here? Aren't you supposed to be in class?"

Miya's hands were too sweaty to hold onto her laptop. She set it on one of the student desks. "I didn't mean to sneak up on you. I called your name at the door, but you didn't hear me. I have a pass from my study hall teacher."

Mr. Callahan bent down and picked up his spoon. When he tossed it into the bowl, brown soup splattered on his desk. He stared at it and turned back to her. "You need to learn to speak up. What is it you want?"

Miya almost said she didn't want anything. She avoided looking at Mr. Callahan's angry eyes behind his thick, black-rimmed glasses and asked her question.

"You said we could retake tests that we failed for partial credit. I'm ready to take tests one and two, please?"

"Do you really think you'll pass them this time? Because I don't want to waste my planning period." Mr. Callahan pulled out a handful of tissues and scrubbed at the gooey brown mess on his desk.

Miya wiped her palms down the front of her jeans. "I'm ready." She wanted to say that she was ready only because Abigail had become the real math teacher, but she kept her mouth shut.

"Well, sit right there while I load the tests."

Miya hesitated. The desk he pointed to belonged to Keefer Jeffries, one of the snarkiest math kids around. She started back to her own seat.

Mr. Callahan didn't look up. "Miya, sit."

After a moment of hesitation, she sat, wishing she'd never come in the first place. Miya stared down at Keefer's desk. The shiny, brown desktop stared back at her.

"Well, don't just sit there. Log in."

Startled, Miya opened her laptop. Mr. Callahan's fingers drummed on his desk as he waited for Miya to enter her six-digit login number. Miya swallowed. She felt her ears turning red at the tips. She knew that number by heart, but under Mr. Callahan's glare, she couldn't remember it. She closed her eyes and rubbed her forehead. The number seven appeared behind her eyelids. She typed it as her fingers remembered the rest.

The first test came up on the screen. Miya read the directions and looked at the first problem. She could do this. Just as Miya began to balance the equation, she heard a rip. Miya looked up. Mr. Callahan unwrapped a supersize Kit Kat bar, the kind you share with a friend.

Miya's mouth started to water. She liked Kit Kat bars. She liked Snickers better, but Kit Kats were an excellent substitute in a stressful situation. She could smell the deliciousness from fourteen feet away. She imagined the creamy milk chocolate melting on her tongue.

"Why aren't you working? You only have 45 minutes left." Mr. Callahan laid the chocolate bar down on his desk and wiped his fingers on a tissue.

Miya didn't answer. She focused on her screen. She needed to ignore him. She needed to do this for herself and for Abigail who'd spent so much time teaching her. Step-by-step, like Abigail had taught her, Miya worked her way carefully through both exams. She didn't have time to go back and check her math, but she understood all the questions and tried them all, even the bonus ones.

When she finished, it took Mr. Callahan less than a minute to score the exams. An 82% and an 84%.

Miya beamed.

"I'll post these scores beside your failing grades." He took out a large white handkerchief and blew his nose loudly. "At least I saw with my own eyes that you didn't cheat."

Miya's smile faded. Heat crawled up her neck.

Step up. Stand up.

"I don't need to cheat." Miya pushed herself out of Keefer's desk. "And I won't fail anymore. I've been working hard with Abigail, and she's been doing *your* job. Oh, and as you can see . . ." Miya pointed to her screen. "She's really good at it because she cares."

Miya snapped her laptop shut, spun on her heel, and stamped down the aisle between the desks. Her heart pounded. How had those words come out of her mouth? She only meant to say the part about not cheating. Miya managed to escape the room before he could respond. She knew her escape was only temporary. Tomorrow was the midterm.

MIYA'S DREAM

* * *

When the girls opened the door to Abigail's kitchen, the smell of freshly baked chocolate chip cookies greeted them. Miya filled her lungs with the scent of butter, brown sugar, and gooey chocolate. Lisa leaned against the counter, transferring cookies from a wire rack to a cookie jar shaped like a chubby black and white cow.

Abigail hugged her grandma and went to the refrigerator. She pulled out a plastic pitcher of red Kool-Aid and poured three glasses. When Lisa finished transferring the cookies, Miya carried the cookie jar over to the table, her mouth watering. She wanted to stick her head in it and inhale, like a bear with a honey pot.

Lisa hobbled over, and the three sat down. Their chairs scraped over the cracked linoleum. They each took a cookie although Miya wanted two. Lisa broke hers in half and said, "Abigail tells me you entered a barrel race on Saturday."

Miya's foot jiggled up and down, up and down. Her hand tightened on the glass. "Yes. Jake convinced me to jump in and get a run under my belt. Now that I signed up, I'm scared to death." Miya looked at her hand. The cookie was gone. She'd inhaled it while jiggling her foot. Miya had hardly tasted it.

Lisa sipped her Kool-Aid. "It's normal to be nervous. I know you and Dream will do just fine."

"That's exactly what I told her," said Abigail. "Grandma, can we go watch Jake and Miya ride Saturday?"

"I don't see why not." Lisa held up her glass. "I'd like to propose a toast: to smooth runs and tight turns."

They all clinked glasses and drank. Abigail wiped the Kool-Aid mustache off with her arm. "Grandma, do you think you should watch Miya practice one more time and give her some last-minute advice?"

"I could do that, I suppose, if Miya wants me to."

Miya froze. *No. No. No.*

Lisa's old-fashioned suggestions would slow her down. Abigail didn't understand that barrel racers in the olden days did stuff different than they do today. So much slower. Miya didn't want to be laughed at.

Miya cleared her throat. "Umm . . . Uh . . . I don't think I'll really have time to do that before the run Saturday. Maybe the next time, though." She stared at the ring her glass left on the table, unwilling to meet Lisa's eyes.

"Of course," said Lisa. "Whenever you'd like."

Miya needed to get Abigail out of the kitchen before she said something else awkward. She jumped to her feet. "Come on, Abigail. We'd better get going. We've got a lot of ground to cover for the midterm tomorrow."

Abigail nodded and put the glasses in the sink. "Thanks for the cookies, Grandma."

"Yes, thank you." Miya swept some crumbs off the table and into her hand. She brushed them off in the trash. Miya grabbed her backpack and hurried up the stairs. As soon as she got to Abigail's room, Miya flung herself into the green camping chair. It squeaked and groaned under her weight. Her cheeks burned as she booted up her computer and opened the review folder. She hoped she hadn't hurt Lisa or Abigail's feelings. Navigating this barrel-racing thing was harder than she thought, and she hadn't even been in her first rodeo.

CREAK. The frayed camp chair squeaked more loudly as Miya settled into it. She scooted closer to the card table but was careful not to lean on it. Miya imagined the table collapsing and both laptops crashing to the floor.

Abigail opened the window. A clean, cool breeze that smelled like Russian olive trees and damp cottonwood leaves blew in. It rippled the pages of Miya's math notebook. She looked down.

"I think I know how to do this one."

Abigail turned her attention to the first review question. As they worked, Miya started to feel better, stronger. She was getting it. She could do it. It helped that when she went to class, Miya paid better attention instead of just wishing it were over. She'd started to listen more carefully in her other classes, too. She reread her assignments and actually studied for the quizzes.

Miya finished a problem and watched Abigail's face as she checked it. Abigail beamed. "Great! You got another one right, and it was hard!"

Miya returned Abigail's smile. "Thanks for helping me with this. You're a real friend. Unlike Lily."

Abigail shrugged. "I like to help people." She frowned. "I'm sorry Lily's not your friend anymore. Is it because she wants to get Jake from you?"

"Jake's not mine!" Miya felt a blush creep up her neck. She cleared her throat. "She's just mad. Let's try the next problem." As Miya scrolled through the review packet, her stomach growled.

Abigail giggled. "Are you hiding a gator in there? Want to feed it some chocolate chip cookies?"

"No, no, no." Miya planned to sneak out without facing Lisa. Her eyes fell on the photograph of baby Abigail. "So . . . what made you guys decide to move here from Montana?"

Abigail walked over and picked up the framed photo. The setting sun streamed in the window and pooled around her as a breeze ruffled her wispy brown hair. "Mom and Dad were coming back from Alaska to help Grandpa with the ranch. After the plane crash, Grandma said Grandpa worked even harder. According to her, he worked himself to death. The bank got the ranch. Grandma, though, she's tough. Toughest person I know. I never saw her cry until the day she put Sprint up for sale."

Miya's eyes widened. "You had to sell Sprint? He's right down there in your pasture. Did you buy him back?"

Abigail's eyes didn't leave the photo. "Luckily, we didn't have to sell him after all. Grandpa's sister, Ida Mann, died and left him this place. I guess it sat empty for a while until the lawyers worked things out and found Grandma. We packed everything in that old truck and prayed it would make it. That's how we ended up here."

Tears gathered at the corners of Miya's eyes. Abigail had been through so much, and her life was still so much harder than Miya's. Lots of kids still teased Abigail about her hair, her clothes, and her glasses. Miya shuddered. She wished she had enough money to buy new frames for Abigail.

Abigail set the picture back on the nightstand. She rubbed her finger across the top of the frame. "Something good came out of losing the ranch." She looked up and smiled. "I found you for a friend."

Her throat tight, Miya smiled back. "Seems to me that you got cheated. You got a friend, but I got a friend *and* a math tutor. Let's do one more problem before I go."

* * *

The next day Miya slid into her seat in math class. She got out her laptop and booted it up. She kept her eyes down. She and

148

Mr. Callahan hadn't even glanced at each other since yesterday when she'd told him he wasn't doing his job.

Miya stared at the screen and frowned. In the movies when someone stood up to a bully, that person magically became stronger, happier, and more confident. The bullies were sorry and changed their ways. There was always a happy ending.

But after she stood up to Mr. Callahan, Miya felt more miserable than ever. She had learned long ago that trouble followed her whenever she drew attention to herself. Winning the shot put two years ago got her the nickname Mega Miya, but that was nothing compared to telling off a teacher, a teacher whose class she was close to failing.

Miya swallowed hard against the desire to throw up.

Mr. Callahan walked up and down the aisle, carrying a basket. He watched as each student, including Miya, dropped their cellphones into the basket. His voice droned on, lecturing about cheating. Miya's stomach gurgled, and sweat gathered on her neck. She glanced at Abigail, who offered a smile and a thumbs up. Miya nodded and pressed her forearm against her stomach as the test came up on the screen. Miya got to work and didn't look up until the bell rang and her screen went blank.

At lunchtime, the smell of oils, acrylics, and glue welcomed Miya as she stepped inside the art room. Country music blared over the speakers with its usual ear-splitting volume. Miya wondered if Mr. O would stream some other kind of music if she asked him. She felt desperate enough to think that soft rock would make a good change.

Miya looked up from unpacking the turkey sandwiches when Abigail walked in. Abigail stopped to admire Isabel's weaving before she made her way over to their table.

"Hey." Abigail picked up a sandwich and peeked inside the ziplock. "Yum, turkey. Before I do another unforgettable landscape, I'm going to see if the math scores have been posted. Do you want me to check yours?"

Miya took out two oranges and two bags of fruit snacks. She didn't want to find out her score yet, but she wouldn't be able to concentrate on her sculpture until she knew. She thought she'd done okay, but she'd thought that before and ended up with a 37%. Miya bit her lip and tasted blood.

"Okay. Do it."

Abigail quickly typed in Miya's login information. Across the room, Miya watched Mr. O's toe tap along with the music. Abigail's face was unreadable as she watched the screen. Miya's toe started to tap, but not in time to the music.

"What does it say?"

Abigail frowned. "Mmm. Let me try that again."

Miya's toe tapped faster, and she drummed her fingers on the table.

"Finally. It's up."

Miya held her breath.

"Yes!" Abigail clapped. "A 92%. Your highest score ever."

Miya slid into the chair, weak with relief. How in the world did she manage a 92%? It had to be a mistake. She was the one who barely scraped through.

"Wait. There's a note from Mr. Callahan."

Miya's stomach clenched. She knew it. The 92 was a mistake.

"'Impressive growth. Keep working with Abigail and you might even pass this class.'" Abigail made a face. "What a jerk."

Miya straightened back up in her chair. As far as she was concerned, Mr. Callahan could say anything he wanted. She got a 92%! She worked hard and earned that score. Maybe she'd earn a good time at the barrel race Saturday.

"So, what did you get on the test?"

Abigail looked up, her cheeks pink. "Actually . . ." She paused and then went on hurriedly. "A 110%."

"A 110%. You got both bonus questions right?" She shook her head, still smiling. "How do you do it? Math is so hard."

"I love numbers." Abigail looked around the art room. "Numbers are my medium of choice. I know, I'll hide some numbers in my picture today. That ought to surprise Mr. O." She went off in search of supplies.

Miya retrieved her sculpture from the closet and carefully, almost reverently, put it on the table. For three days, she'd been trying to get Dream's face right. Her nostrils, her veins, her eyes. Her head was the essence of Dream. Maybe she'd get closer today.

Chapter Nineteen

At 2:00 a.m., Miya slipped her phone under her pillow and closed her eyes. They were gritty from watching dozens of barrel racing videos. Now, she felt even more discouraged than when she'd told her parents goodnight at 10:00 p.m. The barrel racers demonstrated lots of training tips, but none that would help her tomorrow. Miya flipped back and forth in bed, her sheets twisted in a knot.

She'd scratch from the race first thing in the morning. She'd lose her entry fee, but who cared? She needed more time to practice. Lots more time before that blonde on the palomino and the other barrel racers could watch her run. If she ran today, they'd all laugh at her. They'd never accept her. They'd never be her friends in high school next year.

Miya flopped onto her back and stared into the darkness. How would she explain to Jake, her parents, Abigail, and Lisa? Miya groaned and rechecked her phone. 2:30 a.m.

If she went to sleep right now, she'd get three hours of sleep. Maybe exhaustion could be her excuse. Miya tore the top sheet off the bed and threw it onto the floor. This was all Jake's fault—him and his dumb pep talks.

Since she couldn't sleep, Miya thought she might as well go out to the barn and check on Dream. She sat up and reached for her jeans and hoodie. Miya dressed quietly and slipped her phone into her pocket.

Cowboy boots in hand, Miya crept down the stairs. Zoey, curled up on her bed in the kitchen, bounced to her feet and shook. Her tags *CLINK-CLANKED* together.

"Shhh."

Zoey scrambled under the kitchen table and came out with her ball. "No playing ball now," Miya whispered. Miya held open the screen door, and Zoey, tennis ball in her mouth, followed Miya out onto the porch. Miya sat on the steps to pull on her boots, and Zoey dropped the ball in front of her.

"Okay. I'll throw it just once." Miya threw the ball across the barnyard. It landed somewhere in the darkness, and Zoey bounded after it. She brought it back and dropped it at Miya's feet.

Miya leaned against the porch. "Zoey. Zoey. What did your dumb owner get herself into?"

Miya stepped onto the path and looked up at the sky. Millions of white dots swirled across the darkness. *Maybe,* Miya thought, *God is awake right now and using glitter paint to decorate the sky.*

All Miya could do was her best. She nodded. Yes, her best. Would her best be good enough? She knelt down and pulled Zoey closer, hugging her neck. Zoey licked Miya's cheek. Miya hugged her harder. After a long moment, Miya stood up and continued down the path to the barn.

Once Miya reached the barn, she flipped on the single light. The moths started circling it immediately.

ZAP. ZAP. ZAP. The moths smacked into the bulb, and Miya pictured them sprinkling brown moth powder on everything below. One fell to the ground, and Zoey licked it up.

"Yuck, Zoey. That's disgusting." Zoey looked back at the light. "I know you wish another moth treat will fall from the heavens," Miya continued, looking up at the light with Zoey. "If you eat too many, you're gonna be sick."

Dream leaned over her stall door and nickered. Miya walked along the aisle. She skirted the wheelbarrow and passed the red plastic bucket that she'd forgotten to put away yesterday. Miya reached the door of Dream's stall. She rubbed Dream's forehead, and Dream pushed against her hand.

While she loosely braided Dream's forelock, Miya said, "Dream, I'm not gonna lie. This is the most scared I've ever been. When it's my turn, I'll be shaking so hard I won't be able to hold onto the reins. I don't think I can get out of it unless I break a bone or something."

Dream snuffled in Miya's pockets, hoping to find a treat. Miya dug down and found an alfalfa cube, partially covered with dryer lint. She rubbed the lint off and then asked Dream, "Do you have any ideas how I can get out of this?"

Dream's whiskers whispered across Miya's palm as she accepted the treat and blew gently.

"I'll take that as a no." Miya sighed. "I'll get the brushes. With all the time I have to groom you, you might not be the fastest horse there, but you'll be the shiniest."

* * *

A restless wind rattled the sign wired to the gate: **WARNING: Ride at Your Own Risk**. The wind skipped across the mud puddles, causing the riders to jam cowboy hats down more tightly over ponytails and braids.

Miya stood beside Dream, a short distance away from the other barrel racers. She'd asked her family to wait in the stands until she ran. Miya didn't want the other girls to think she was a baby who needed her daddy to stand beside her. Now, she wished he were here. He and Jake both.

Miya imagined Mom and Jake's mom sitting in the bleachers, chit-chatting with their fingers crossed for her. Her dad and Jake's dad would be talking about turning on the irrigation water next week. Lisa and Abigail would huddle together. Lisa probably had a program and would keep track of the barrel racers' times. Abigail would be tapping her foot in her blue, plastic shoes. Leaning back against the bleachers, Jake and Julia would be laughing.

Julia! Miya couldn't believe it when Dream's former owner had pulled into the arena parking lot this morning. Miya had been unloading Dream when she looked up and saw Julia getting out of her dad's sweet rodeo truck. Miya's stomach had dropped so low it hit her boots. Julia was all smiley and nice while thanking Dad for inviting her. Miya froze in place.

Miya bent down and checked Dream's splint boots. Satisfied that the Velcro was still snug, Miya stood back up and chewed the inside of her mouth. Miya wished she could make her first run without an audience. She was afraid that she'd disappoint all of her family and friends and let Dream down.

Miya turned her attention to the other barrel racers. They waited on a strip of rocky ground that bordered the rodeo parking lot. Miya could hardly stand to watch the other girls enter the alley. They looked confident and professional. She and Dream weren't ready yet.

Miya needed to use the restroom again, but the port-a-potty was too far away. She imagined the announcer calling her name while she was inside. Miya imagined herself frantically pulling up her jeans and climbing on Dream as the port-a-potty door slammed behind her. No, thank you. She'd hold it.

Dream touched Miya's arm with her nose. Miya jumped and then rubbed Dream's neck.

"Hi, Dream. I have something for us to share." Miya reached into her jacket pocket for a Hershey bar. She tore it open and stuffed the paper back into her pocket. Miya broke the candy bar in two and offered half to Dream. Miya scratched her forehead, working her fingers under Dream's headstall to reach the sweaty places.

"The candy will help calm our nerves." Miya took a bite from her half and let the chocolate melt on her tongue. She was thankful that the order of the jackpot was switched today. Barrel racing would be first instead of bull riding. It was hard enough to wait for the other barrel racers to run, let alone watch all the bull riders.

The announcer's voice crackled over the loudspeakers. "Miya Skippingbird. Be getting it on your mind."

Miya Skippingbird! That was her name. Getting it on her mind meant that there were only three more girls before her. Panicked, Miya jerked Dream's cinch to tighten it. Dream snorted.

"Sorry, sorry," Miya said, patting Dream's shoulder and loosening it a notch.

"Miya Skippingbird in the hole."

In the hole? Only two more contestants and it was her turn. Miya tugged on her waistband and worked her foot up to the stirrup. She flung herself up on Dream. Surprised, Dream stepped to the side.

"Sorry, sorry," Miya said, again. She bent down to slip her rubber bands over her toes and around her stirrups.

"Miya Skippingbird on deck."

On deck? She was next. She got the rubber band on her left foot, but she couldn't get the other one over her right toe. Miya knew she needed both rubber bands around her toes and heels to keep her feet in the stirrups when she ran. Why hadn't she let Dad wait with her? He'd have slipped the rubber bands on, and she wouldn't be panicking now.

"Miya Skippingbird. You're up!"

Oh, no!

She threw the rubber band on the ground. It was her turn. With the left rubber band on, she'd have to make do.

MIYA'S DREAM

Miya's breaths were quick and shallow as she and Dream started down the alley. About halfway down, she felt her shoulders relax. It was a relief to finally be running! With each of Dream's strides, exhilaration flooded through her.

Wow, she was actually doing this! Dream sensed Miya's excitement and pulled at the bit, wanting to go faster. Although they were still a distance from the starting line, Miya loosened up on her reins. Dream leaped forward, gathering speed.

When they entered the arena, the ground changed. The alley had been hard-packed, but the arena itself was worked up and deep. It had been watered—a little too much because the mud sucked at Dream's feet. Dream struggled through it, slowing her pace. Miya rocked back and forth in the saddle. They were taking forever to reach the first barrel! Dream had to go faster! Miya tapped her with her whip. A couple of light taps on her butt. Dream responded by surging forward—straight past the first barrel instead of turning it.

Miya hauled back on the reins. Dream dropped back to a trot and rounded the first barrel. Miya kicked her again. "Come on, Dream. Let's make a good turn on the next two barrels." Dream started running again, awkwardly through the deep mud. Dream swung wide but managed to get around the second barrel at a lope. Miya was so focused on the turns that she forgot to keep enough pressure in her stirrups. As Dream came out of the second barrel, Miya's foot slipped out of her right stirrup. Miya tried to find it without looking down.

Dream was tired, but she ran as hard as she could to the third barrel. Miya stared at it, still trying to get her foot into the stirrup. They were almost there.

As Miya struggled with the stirrup, Dream ran where Miya's body told her to go. To the barrel, not to the side of it. Dream knocked the barrel over with her shoulder as she tried to turn it. A five-second penalty. Miya saw the barrel roll to the ground out of the corner of her eye. How could it have happened so quickly? Miya closed her eyes and opened them, staring down at her saddle horn. A tear plopped onto the middle of it. A horrible way to end a horrible run.

Head still down, fighting back an avalanche of tears, Miya jogged Dream toward the gate.

The speaker crackled to life. "28.79 for that cowgirl."

Miya's heart broke into a thousand sharp pieces. She knew it was bad, but that bad? No applause sounded from the crowd. Miya avoided the gateman's eyes and kept trotting straight back to the trailer.

When she arrived, Miya reached down and pulled the left rubber band off her boot. She wrapped it around her saddle horn. Miya stepped off Dream and petted her neck. "Thanks for trying so hard, girl. I messed up. Not you."

Miya pulled off Dream's splint boots when a pair of tennis shoes and a pair of cowboy boots stopped beside her. Miya refused to look up.

"Miya, honey, I'm sorry," said the voice belonging to the tennis shoes.

"Mom," Miya said. "This is the worst day of my life. I want to go home."

The voice of the cowboy boots said, "Hey now, you didn't do so bad on the second barrel."

Miya sniffled. "Not so bad? The whole thing was horrible. I'm never running again."

The cowboy boots shuffled. "Miya, don't say that. We can leave, but don't you want to stay until Jake rides?"

"No, Dad. I don't. Mr. Star Athlete will do just fine without me in the stands. Let's go."

Miya pulled off Dream's saddle and lugged it to the tack compartment. Mom filled a bucket and offered Dream a drink of water. Dad buckled a light sheet on Dream, and Miya led her into the trailer.

Miya climbed into the truck and hugged herself tightly. Her parents got in on either side of her. She cringed, thinking about Lisa in the stands. Lisa, a champion, watched Miya make a huge mess of things. Maybe she should've listened to Lisa better. It didn't matter now. Miya was never going to barrel race again. Never.

Chapter Twenty

After Miya turned Dream out into the pasture, she snuck into the house, changed into her soft, ratty sweats, and curled up under her quilt. Zoey whined at the door.

"Go away, Zoey," Miya said without getting up. She didn't need Zoey's scratching and snoring right now.

Miya burrowed deeper into her bed. She started counting backward.

100, 99, 98 . . .

Miya's cheeks burned. Why had she let Dream run so hard down the alley? Dream was tired before she got to the first barrel. Poor Dream. That mare kept on trying, though, even when Miya used her whip at the wrong time and drove her past the first barrel. Miya focused on the numbers to erase the painful images.

97, 96, 95 . . .

She should call Julia and have her pick up Dream. Miya didn't deserve Dream. Tears ran down her cheeks. She pressed the edge of her quilt against her eyes, but the tears kept flowing.

Zoey whined and scratched at the door. Miya threw the quilt aside and went to the door. She opened it wide enough for Zoey to squeeze through. Miya climbed back into bed, and Zoey jumped beside her.

"Zoey, I was so stupid to ignore Lisa." Miya choked on another sob. "I should have ignored all the advice online and listened to someone who could work with me and Dream. Now it's too late. I'll never go over to Abigail's house again. Never."

MIYA'S DREAM

Zoey licked Miya's face and curled up against Miya's legs. *78,77,76 . . .*
Somewhere around *30*, Miya drifted off.

* * *

The buzzing of her phone woke Miya. She lay still for a second, wondering why she was in bed in the afternoon. Then, she remembered the barrel race. Tears trickled down her cheeks. She swiped at them with the corner of her quilt.

Miya reached for her phone and saw a message from Lily.

I sent something to Skylar to post. I tagged you.

Miya opened the app on her phone to see that Skylar had posted the video of Miya's run.

Skylar
#MegaMiyacomesinlast #whataloser
"Don't watch it," Miya told herself. "Delete it."

Yet her thumb pressed the play arrow. Lily narrated her run with colorful commentary and OMGs. By the third barrel, Lily was laughing too hard to talk.

Miya needed to stop the video, get rid of it, and close her account. She should put down her phone, but her thumb began scrolling through the comments—all 52 of them.

Kaylee
The poor horse is having a heart attack.

Ava
He should be riding Mega Miya, not the other way around.

Hannah
Give her a Walmart scooter. They were made for wide loads.

Cathy Ringler

The comments became too blurry when she tried to read them again. Miya curled up under her quilt, hoping to muffle her sobs.

* * *

Monday morning, Miya dragged herself through the halls. Groups of kids laughed at her as she walked by. Two boys in ballcaps walked down the hall, bouncing a basketball back and forth to each other. Skylar Peters held hands with Mitchell, and as soon as she caught sight of Miya, she giggled.

"Giddyap, Miya," she said.

"I'm surprised you didn't pull that horse over on top of you when you went around those barrels," said Mitchell.

Miya's cheeks burned. She kept her head down as she shuffled along the worn floor. The video had been shared over and over that weekend and had collected more comments, comments Miya couldn't keep herself from reading.

Kaitlyn
A hippo on horseback.
Kaylee
OMG! I can't stop laughing.
Jake hurried over. "Hey."
Miya answered without looking up. "Hey."
"I missed you on the bus today." Jake shifted his backpack.
"Mom drove me."

Miya plodded toward the math classroom, and Jake fell into step beside her. The giggling continued, but the comments stopped. At the classroom door, Jake squeezed her hand before heading down the hall.

Miya sank down into her chair and rubbed her thumb back and forth over her palm. She wished Jake could walk with her all day. She booted up her computer. She stared at the red, green, and purple swirls on the screen.

"Hi, Miya," said Mr. Callahan. He had never even acknowledged her presence, and now he greeted her?

Miya looked up, surprised. "Hi."

"Were you able to get your homework done last night?"

Miya looked back at the screen. "No."

"If you can get it in by the end of the day, I'll give you full credit. You're climbing into the B zone. I'd hate to see you jeopardize that by missing assignments."

Miya shrugged and kept her eyes on her computer.

* * *

The sun streamed in through the big window in the art room. A single bright shaft fell on an almost finished batik. The blues and purples of the peaks bathed in golden sunlight touched the dark place inside her. Miya stared at the artwork on the fabric for a long time. Maybe she'd try it one day.

Mr. O strolled over, humming bits and pieces of the country song that blared over the speakers. "Miya, I baked your sculpture last night, and I think you'll be pleased with how it turned out. I am."

Miya followed Mr. O to the cart by the oven. Her eyes skipped over the beige Star Wars and cartoon figures the other students had made. They were arranged in a circle, forming a protective ring around Dream. Miya stared. Her mouth opened. Closed. Opened again.

"It's . . . it's . . ."

"Fantastic." Mr. O finished with a grin.

The pain in Miya's heart pulled back a bit, like a bandage being slowly worked off a scab. The weeks of learning to use the embossing tools, needles, spatulas, and blades paid off. Somehow, she managed to capture the heart of Dream. Maybe it was through her neck and pricked-up ears. Maybe it appeared in the lines of her head or the curve of her back. It was inexplicable, but it was Dream running with grace and courage.

Mr. O started to say something else. He stopped when he noticed students boiling water at the batik station. "I'll be back," he said and hurried away. Miya carefully picked up the sculpture and moved it to her table. She stood back and admired it again.

Abigail came up behind her. "Oh, wow."

"I know, right? I don't know how it happened. I could never do it again. It's Dream."

A pink gym bag slammed across the table. Lily stood next to Miya and Abigail, her arms crossed, her jaw drawn tight. After inching her gym bag closer to the sculpture, Lily smiled and recrossed her arms.

Lily glanced at the sculpture and turned to Abigail and Miya. "How did you like the video Skylar posted?"

Miya's happiness with the sculpture, as clean as pine-scented air, vanished. She clenched her fists.

"Why did you send that video to Skylar?"

"Duh, I'm her friend now. And friends stick together, right? Oh, wait. You wouldn't know." Lily studied her painted black fingernails on one hand.

Miya opened her mouth, but she couldn't remember a word of the speech she'd rehearsed in her mind a hundred times as she'd lain in bed and cried.

Abigail stepped between them. "Go away, Lily. What you did was terrible. Miya doesn't need a friend like you."

Lily's smirk grew. "And I don't need loser friends like you two. Hide in here all you want, Miya. Even if you came back to the cafeteria, I wouldn't eat lunch with you anymore. I hang out with Skylar and her friends now."

Lily picked up her gym bag and slung it over her shoulder. As she spun toward the door, her bag slammed into the sculpture of Dream. Miya gasped as the sculpture shattered against the floor.

All three girls froze. Lily moved first. As she threaded her way through the easels and potter's wheels, she turned to look back once. Her wide eyes found Miya's, but quickly looked away. With a shaking hand, Lily opened the door a crack and slipped out.

Dream lay in pieces on the art room floor—head twisted, legs broken, and tail missing.

Miya covered her face with her hands as she dropped to her knees. From far away, she could hear someone making a strange noise—half-scream, half-sob. She felt Abigail's hands on her shoulders.

"Don't cry, Miya," Abigail said. "Don't cry."

Mr. O was there saying something, but Miya couldn't make out the words. The sobbing, screaming noise was too loud.

Isabel, the red-haired weaving girl, came over. She carefully pried Miya's hands off her eyes. "Shh-shh-shh," she said over and over as she hugged Miya. Her voice mingled with Miya's sobs like the warp and weft of the hangings she wove.

After wiping her eyes, Miya looked closer at Isabel. A yellow string of yarn stuck to Isabel's bangs. Once again, Miya covered her face with her hands. Another flood of sobs shook her.

Isabel hugged and patted Miya's back while Abigail explained the broken sculpture to Mr. O. He walked to his office, and after a few minutes, his boots *CLIP-CLOPPED* back to Miya. Miya's sobs quieted to hiccups. With Abigail's and Isabel's help, she stood.

Mr. O rested his hand on her shoulder. "I called your mom. She's coming to pick you up. I cleared it with the office. I'm so sorry, Miya."

Miya nodded. Tears dripped off her nose. Miya felt a wave of helplessness so strong that she staggered backward and almost fell to her knees again. Her life felt like that ruined sculpture—broken, shattered pieces covering the ground. One piece was "Mega Miya." Another was the video with all of the shares and comments. Another was barrel racing. Another was math. And another was . . . She shook her head and started to sob again.

Abigail gently pulled Miya's hand. "C'mon. Your mom will be here in a minute." Miya allowed herself to be led to the door. Her legs felt so heavy Miya barely had the strength to put one foot in front of the other. She glanced back as she left. Mr. O was on his knees beside Dream.

Chapter Twenty-One

The setting sun's too-bright light peeked its way into Miya's bedroom, but Miya didn't have the energy to get up and close the curtains. Her arms and legs felt like lead encased her bones. Grit filled her eyes. Her limp hair spread over the pillow.

The smell of macaroni and cheese didn't interest her. Mom had made her special homemade recipe to try to cheer her up, but Miya hadn't eaten it. The food had been sitting on her desk for over an hour now. The meal Mom had left last night had received the same treatment—untouched, unwanted.

A knock sounded at the door.

Miya remained silent, hoping the knocker would go away.

Another knock and the door opened.

Zoey darted into the room, Mom following closely behind. Zoey flopped down on Miya's fluffy blue throw rug and scratched energetically.

Mom perched on the side of the bed. She smoothed Miya's hair away from her face and put her hand on Miya's forehead.

"Miya, honey. Look at me."

Miya unwillingly opened her eyes.

"I would do anything in my power to take this pain away from you." Mom smoothed the corner of Miya's quilt. "But, baby, you've been up here for three days, and now it's time to come out and get going again."

Tears trickled from the corners of Miya's eyes. She thought she'd run out of tears, but apparently not. "I'm so tired," she whispered.

Mom leaned over and kissed Miya's forehead. "I get that you're tired. Growing up is hard, and right now you can't see

Cathy Ringler

past your hurt. Take it from someone who's been through several storms. This, too, will pass."

Miya squeezed her eyes shut to hold back a fresh wave of tears. Miya nodded. Mom touched Miya's arm lightly and then stood. She picked up the plates with Miya's untouched supper, whispered "Love you," and disappeared into the hallway.

Mom didn't get it. What would pass? The ache of losing something beautiful that she'd never be able to create again? Lily, Skylar, and all the other kids who hated her at school? Never barrel running again and letting Dream down? Jake finding a prettier, skinnier girlfriend cuz Miya couldn't work up the nerve to tell him she liked him?

Miya was tired. Tired of wondering. Tired of wishing. Tired of fighting. She closed her eyes and drifted off into a fitful sleep.

* * *

Miya woke with a start. Footsteps caused the stairs to squeak. She picked up her phone to see a bright 4:30 p.m. shining at her. She'd slept another day away.

A quick knock came through the door. Before Miya could answer, it flew open, and Mom appeared in the doorway. Zoey slipped into the room.

"You have a visitor," Mom announced in a cheery voice. Mom threw open the window.

Miya didn't turn away from the wall. "I don't want to see anyone."

"Too bad, Miya, cuz I want to see you."

Jake! She didn't want him to see her like this, hair greasy and tangled. When had she showered last? She couldn't do anything about it now. Jake leaned against the doorframe looking perfect, as always.

Miya yanked the quilt up under her chin. "Go away."

"Not gonna happen."

Mom pushed her sleeves up her arms. "I'm starting dinner. Call if you need anything." She smiled at Jake as she left, leaving the door to Miya's room wide open.

Miya squeezed her eyes shut. Her computer chair squeaked as Jake settled into it. He whistled, and Zoey's nails clicked across the floor to where he sat.

Miya needed to get rid of him.

She heard the computer chair shift and Jake's laughter. "Zoey, you're too big to sit in my lap. Get down." **A rustle.** *CLUNK.* Zoey must have slid to the floor. Jake started whistling. The sound grated on Miya's nonexistent patience.

Miya sighed. "Okay. Talk."

"Don't mind if I do. Miya, you're my best friend. I miss you on the bus. I miss seeing you at school. I just plain miss you."

Miya opened her eyes and sat up. Instead of looking at Jake, she focused on the wall behind him, on the crayon horse picture she'd drawn. At five years old, she'd worked on it with a flashlight for over a week after she'd been put to bed. It didn't look too bad. But now, after losing her sculpture, Miya would never, ever create another horse. Not sketched, painted, or molded. No more horses.

"I can't go back, Jake. I don't belong there. I'm gonna see if Mom will homeschool me."

"Nope. Nope. Stop thinking like that Miya. You have to go back and face them. You're one of the bravest people I know. You can't leave until you finish what you started."

"What did I start?"

"That would be eighth grade."

"I'm not brave. I'm so tired of being laughed at, of being 'Mega Miya.' I can't change how those kids see me."

The horse on the wall started to blur as tears gathered in her eyes.

"Quit giving a bunch of kids so much power over you. You are brave. Look how you jumped into your first barrel race." Jake scooted the chair closer to the bed.

Miya remembered Lily's videos and all of the comments attached to it. "I won't be doing that again, either."

"Yes, you will cuz I'm gonna ride with you. We'll work on those drills together."

If Miya had the energy, she would have laughed. "So you're gonna get into barrel racing now?"

"No, but those drills will improve my roping."

Miya sighed. "Bye, Jake. I'm going back to sleep."

She heard the squeak of the chair as he got up.

Jake touched her shoulder lightly. "See you on the bus tomorrow, and Saturday, we ride."

After making certain he'd left, Miya sniffed. Jake was crazy if he thought she'd ever go back to that horrible place.

* * *

Later that evening, Mom reappeared after another quick tap on the door. "You have another visitor."

Miya flopped over so she faced the wall again. What was this? Grand Central Station?

SLAP. SLAP. SLAP. SLAP.

Miya could recognize the sound of Abigail's blue, plastic shoes anywhere.

Miya pretended to be asleep, hoping Abigail would get the hint.

"I know you're playing 'possum. You've been out three days, and I wish you'd come back."

Miya stayed quiet and tried to breathe slowly and steadily, trying to mimic sleep. She wondered if it would be overkill to add a little snore.

Abigail continued. "Math is still math. I'll help you get caught up when you're ready." The computer chair squeaked as she sat down. Abigail began to twirl around in it. Twirling the computer chair faster, she said, "It's weird in the art room without you. Mr. O is letting me help him check off sixth-grade art projects. I think he's given up on my landscapes."

At the mention of the art room, tears climbed the back of Miya's throat. She coughed them away. "People think I'm being a drama queen, but that sculpture was more than just a hunk of clay. It was the only thing I did right this year. And I can't ever get it back." Miya wiped her nose on the quilt. "You don't understand. You don't know how it feels to lose something like that."

Miya heard the computer chair hit the desk with a thud. Abigail's plastic shoes smacked across the floor. She stopped at the foot of Miya's bed.

In between rapid breaths, Abigail said, "Are you really that selfish? Do you think you're the only person on this whole earth who's lost something important to them? News flash, Miya: other people have lost more than you!"

Miya stopped crying.

"But you're right," Abigail continued. "I didn't lose *things*. I lost the three most important people in the world. No more Dad to tease me. No more Mom to kiss goodnight. No more Grandpa to do chores with. Then, I lost the ranch, the place I used to play hide-and-seek, the place I played with my kittens. As if that wasn't enough, we had to move here, and I lost all the friends I've had since kindergarten. *Real* friends who don't make fun of me because I don't dress like a supermodel. Don't you dare whine to me about loss, Miya. I'm way ahead of you in that department."

SLAP. SLAP. SLAP. Abigail's shoes headed toward the door. Miya threw off her quilt, jumped out of bed, and tripped over Zoey.

"Wait, Abigail! Wait! You're right. You are so right." She grabbed Abigail's arm. "I'm sorry. *Really* sorry. I can't believe I said that."

Abigail allowed herself to be led over to the computer chair, and Miya sat on the edge of the bed. "Me and my big mouth. You're my friend. I don't want to lose you, too."

Abigail cocked her head to one side, and she tapped her finger against her jaw. After an agonizing moment, she said, "I'll forgive you if you promise to come back to school tomorrow."

Before Miya could answer, a cane thumped on the stairs. Lisa called, "Come on down, Abigail, and bring Miya with you."

Miya looked wide-eyed at Abigail. She couldn't face Lisa.

"Save me," Miya whispered.

Abigail shrugged. "Can't."

Miya wrapped the quilt around her shoulders and started down the stairs. Abigail followed a step behind. When they got to the bottom, Lisa and Mom turned and walked into the kitchen. Miya and Abigail followed.

Lisa motioned to a kitchen chair. "Have a seat, Miya."

Miya sat down. Mom pulled out a chair and sat down, too, cradling a cup of coffee in her hands. Abigail squatted down by Zoey and scratched the dog behind her ears.

Lisa pinched Miya's chin and forced her to look straight into her steely blue eyes.

Lisa broke the silence. "What's this I hear about you giving up on barrel racing?"

Miya sighed and tried to look away, but Lisa's grip held firm. "After what happened last weekend, I don't want to run anymore. I'll never be any good, and it's not fair to Dream."

Lisa snorted and released Miya's chin. "Now if that ain't a bunch of cow puckie, I don't know what is. You got a good little horse, and you're a good rider. You need to get that foundation we talked about right."

Miya sighed. "I can't seem to do anything right."

Lisa leaned her hip against the table. "You can if you're willing to change your attitude, listen to advice, and work hard."

Miya shoved the quilt off her shoulders and straightened in her chair. "I'm sorry for the way I acted before. I'm ready to change. I promise." Miya's heart raced. She took a deep breath and pressed on. "If I help out with chores at your house, would you be willing to help me and Dream build that foundation? I don't want to barrel race, but I want to be the kind of rider Dream deserves."

Lisa nodded. "You go on back to school. Come by the house on Saturday morning. I'll work with you and Abby."

Miya looked at Abigail, surprised. "I thought you were afraid to ride."

"I am." Abigail nodded. "I'm going to attempt to ride Foxy. She'll try to take care of me." Abigail made fists and held up her muscles. "I will be facing my fears."

Miya laughed, but her stomach flipped over. Tomorrow she'd have to face hers.

Chapter Twenty-Two

Mom stood at the counter, making waffles, and she turned as Miya entered the kitchen. "Hi, sweetheart. You look cute in your new shirt."

Miya looked down. "Thanks for buying it for me. It's my favorite color."

"You're welcome." Mom brought a plate of waffles and bacon over to the table. "I made you a special breakfast."

Miya sat down and took a sip of orange juice. "Thanks, Mom." She picked up her knife and put a pat of butter on her waffle. "At least it's Friday. I'm one day closer to the end of the year."

"Yes, you are." Mom sat down across from Miya and took a sip of coffee. "It's good to go back on a Friday. You can get your assignments and work on them over the weekend."

Miya stared at the pool of melted butter on her waffle. "I wish I didn't have to go to school. All the kids will be laughing behind my back. They'll be watching and waiting for me to have another meltdown."

"Oh, honey, maybe not." Mom reached out and touched Miya's arm. "You said there weren't any videos posted. That's a good sign."

Miya poured syrup on her waffle. "If it had to happen, I'm glad it happened in art. Art kids don't post anything mean. They usually put up pictures of their projects." Miya spooned blueberries on top of her waffle. "Speaking of projects, there's a girl named Isabel who does these cool weavings. I'll show you a picture when I get home this afternoon."

Mom took another sip of coffee. "I'd like that. Do you want me to drive you to school?"

While chewing her waffle, Miya considered the offer. Although there seemed to be no videos floating around, everyone would know about Miya's meltdown. She'd have to face whispers, giggles, and curious looks. If Mom drove her to school, Miya could deal with the bus later.

Miya nibbled on a piece of bacon. It would be best to get the entire day over with, and that included the bus ride.

Miya reached for her backpack. "Thanks for the offer and breakfast. I'll go ahead and ride the bus. I have to face it eventually."

Mom stood up and hugged her. "If you need me for any reason at all, just call."

"Thanks, I will." Miya opened the screen door. She and Zoey stepped out onto the porch.

The waffle sat like a stone in her stomach, and her head ached. She rubbed her temples. "I'll put one foot in front of the other until I get through this day," she told Zoey. "Then, I'll put one day behind the other until it's summer."

Miya knelt down and hugged Zoey. "Come on, girl. Now that I got my courage up, I don't want to miss the bus." Side-by-side, they started down the path.

* * *

Jake smiled at Miya as she sat down beside him on the bus. "Glad you're back."

"Thanks." Miya sat down on the plastic, green seat. Instead of setting her backpack on the floor, Miya held it in her lap, hugging it to her chest. Her foot jiggled up and down.

Jake cocked his head and studied her. "You could set that down on the floor."

175

Miya shook her head. "No. I'm good. I just don't feel like talking right now."

"Okay." After giving Miya a light punch on the arm, Jake put his earbuds in.

Miya glanced around the bus. No Lily. She leaned over to Jake, and he slipped his earbuds out. "Lily's not on the bus. That's good."

Jake shrugged. "Maybe, maybe not. Listen, I know Lily's been mean to you, but you gotta give her a break. She's been going through a rough time with the divorce and all."

The seat creaked as she moved away from Jake. "Give her a break? Give *her* a break! After what she did to me? I don't think so."

Jake slipped his earbuds back in, leaned back against the seat, and closed his eyes. "Suit yourself."

Miya stared at him. How could he take Lily's side? He was supposed to be her friend. Miya drummed her fingers against her backpack and then punched Jake's arm—hard. He pulled the earbuds out again.

"What was that for?" he asked, annoyed.

"Why did you say that about Lily? I thought you were on my side."

"I'm not taking sides. That's why I'm telling you to stop thinking of Lily as public enemy number one and start thinking about her as someone who's been through some tough times. If you don't change the way you think about her, you won't be able to move past this."

Jake had a point—maybe.

Miya set her backpack on the floor and faced Jake. "You might be onto something. I'll think about it."

Jake grinned, the dimple appearing in his cheek. "That's a good start." He tugged on her braid. "Good luck today. You can do this."

Miya tried to smile back. She hoped she could.

* * *

Miya hurried down the hall to math. Since she already had her laptop and math notebook, she didn't take the time to stop at her locker. She knew she had a lot to catch up on, and she didn't want to be late.

As she skirted a group of kids in the hall, Miya kept her eyes on the floor. She didn't look back. She didn't want to see who laughed or whispered.

Miya stepped through the door and looked around the empty classroom. Maybe she should've stopped at her locker. Before she could leave, Mr. Callahan saw her and stepped out of his office. Panicking, Miya did the only thing she could. She sat down at her desk and opened her computer. As Mr. Callahan stopped beside her, she braced herself for him to yell at her for all of the missing assignments.

Great. Just great.

"Hey, Miya," Mr. Callahan squatted beside her desk, putting himself at eye level. He never did that. He always towered over her.

"Hey." Miya concentrated on the swirls of the screensaver, waiting for him to start his lecture.

"Mr. O explained what happened. And, um . . ." Miya sucked in a breath. "You can turn in all of your assignments whenever you get them done. I won't dock you."

Miya stared at him in surprise. Behind the thick glasses, his brown eyes looked kind.

Miya blinked. "Thanks. I'll get them done as soon as I can."

"That's fine." Kids filtered into the room, found their seats, and pulled out their laptops. Mr. Callahan stood but hesitated as though he wanted to say something else. He shook his head and walked to the front of the room.

"Students, your attention please."

The talking subsided.

After a few moments, Mr. Callahan said, "I haven't been doing as good a job as you all deserve this year. Someone with courage pointed that out. When you get older, it's harder to admit you need to change. Today, I'm going to try. We'll start class by dividing into groups of two for a math game. Abigail and Miya, you're a group. Nora and Thomas . . ."

After Mr. Callahan finished dividing the class into groups, he explained the game and handed out slips of paper and dice. Miya and Abigail found a quiet corner and set up the board.

Rattling the dice lightly in one hand, Miya said, "I haven't played a game in math since elementary school."

Abigail giggled. "Don't look now, but I think our teacher has been replaced with an alien clone because the real Mr. Callahan would never let us play a math game."

"You could be right," Miya said with a laugh. "Can I come over after school so we can work on some of the stuff I missed?"

"Yeah. We can also work some tomorrow after our riding lessons with Grandma. If I survive the ride, that is."

Miya chose a yellow game marker and watched Mr. Callahan sit on the floor beside a group of four boys. He watched one of them solve an equation, nodded, and moved on to another group.

Miya turned back to Abigail. "Any ideas on where we should eat lunch? Maybe we could take up sewing and go to the home ec room."

"Art room as usual," Abigail said, no longer smiling. "Mr. O said he wanted to talk to you when you got back."

"I don't know if I'm ready to go back to the art room."

Abigail put a green marker on the board. "You gotta go sometime, and you know the art kids are cool."

Miya rolled the dice. The art kids weren't the problem. Miya didn't know if she could face the place where Dream lay shattered on the floor.

* * *

Miya pulled open the art room door. She took a deep breath of air filled with the scents of oils, turpentine, and chalk dust and forced herself to step inside. The now-finished mountain batik drew her attention first. Stretched out in a frame, it shimmered in the sunlight that streamed through the window. Miya tilted her head and wondered how the artist managed to capture just the right shades of blue, purple, and green for the mountains. The result made the work seem effortless and perfectly intentional, but maybe it had happened like her sculpture—a blessed, inexplicable miracle.

Isabel came up beside her and put an arm around her shoulders. "Glad you're back. I just wanted to tell you that your sculpture was beautiful. I'm sorry it broke."

Miya blushed, remembering how this girl had gotten an up-close-and-personal view of her despair. "Thanks." Miya needed to escape. She couldn't talk to Mr. O right now.

As though thinking about him conjured him up, Mr. O appeared between her and the door.

"Miya, thanks for coming by. Let's talk in my office. The music isn't quite so loud there." He started toward the glass cubicle.

Miya tried to explain that she'd come back another day, but the guitars and drums were so loud they drowned out her efforts. Miya shrugged as she walked behind him. Maybe it was best to get this talk over with.

As they entered his office, Miya's glance fell on Mr. O's desk. His computer sat squarely in the middle of it, the screen almost covered with yellow sticky notes. On the shelf above it stood a framed picture of a smiling blond woman and a toddler building a sandcastle. Miya's eyes traveled to a table beside Mr. O's desk. She stared in disbelief. Was this some sort of a cruel trick? She closed her eyes and counted to five. When she reopened her eyes, it didn't disappear. The pieces of her Dream spread out like roadkill.

Blinded by tears, Miya spun around to leave. She nearly bumped into Mr. O, who blocked her way. "Wait, Miya." He pointed to the table. "Calm down and look."

Miya shook her head, flinging her braid back and forth. "No, I won't cuz it's not just some broken pieces of clay laying there. It's me, Mega Miya, knocked down again. I try to stand up and be someone or to create something, and it always gets ruined. I'm done with it. Just leave me alone."

Miya stared at the floor, waiting for Mr. O to step aside, but he didn't move. She focused on the faint music and forced her breathing to slow.

"The thing is, Miya, you promised to finish a sculpture by the end of the semester, and that's what I'm holding you to."

"I tried! You know I *almost* finished. This wasn't my fault!"

"I agree. It wasn't your fault. Nevertheless, I see two choices. You either start building another armature today or repair this one."

Miya forced herself to pick up a piece of the sculpture. The body seemed okay, but a front leg was broken off at the knee. The tail was gone. The head hung loosely off the neck, but otherwise, it was intact. For the first time, she looked at Mr. O.

"Even if I am able to stick it back together, Dream won't be the same."

"No, she won't, but all of us are a little broken. If we pick up the pieces and learn something in the process, we come out stronger." He waited, his black cowboy boot tapping to the beat of the music.

Miya stared at the sculpture. Twisted wire stuck out from the armature of what had once been Dream's leg. Maybe Mr. O was right, maybe her horse didn't need to be precisely the same as long as she came through with her spirit intact.

"Will you help me fix her?"

He smiled. "I'd be honored."

Miya looked out through the smudged glass at the batik. Hope felt like a hummingbird fluttering in her belly. "I'll look up repairing sculptures with polymer clay online."

"Sounds good. I'll brush up on some techniques, too. We'll start tomorrow." Mr. O smiled, crinkling his eyes at the corners. "Now, if we could only get Abigail to draw a decent tree . . ."

Miya laughed. "All we can do is keep trying. Someday, maybe she'll create a forest."

* * *

Saturday dawned with a bright, cloudless day. Miya smiled as she trotted Dream along the wide barrow ditch to Abigail's house. Tiny purple and yellow flowers threaded the green grass. Dream snorted as a killdeer flew a short distance and landed, dragging its wing and hopping across the grass.

CHEEP. CHEEP.

Miya knew that mama killdeers faked injuries to lead predators away from their eggs. She always wondered why killdeers built their nests on the ground. Another one of nature's mysteries.

As she started down Abigail's driveway, she heard laughter. A horse whinnied. Dream pricked up her ears and called back. Hawk, Jake's horse, and Foxy, Abigail's horse, were saddled and tied to the fence. Her friends dragged tires and set up orange cones. Miya saw Jake, and her smile widened. She leaned forward, asking Dream to trot faster. She couldn't wait for the lesson to begin.

When Miya got to the arena, she nearly fell off her horse when she saw Lisa riding Sprint. Lisa wore a checkered long-sleeved shirt, new blue jeans, and polished brown boots. The sun glinted off her world champion buckle. Sprint walked calmly around the arena. He barely glanced at Miya and Dream, his attention focused on his rider.

"Wow, Lisa, you're riding." Miya couldn't keep the surprise out of her voice.

Lisa smiled, and her blue eyes sparkled. "Yep. It wasn't easy to get this old lady in the saddle, but between Jake, Abby, and Lady Luck, we did it. You're going to learn some things today that I'll demonstrate as I teach you. I'll warm up Sprint a bit more. I see Dream is already warmed up from the ride over. We'll start in about five minutes."

Jake and Abigail got on their horses and rode over to Miya. Hawk stretched out his nose and nuzzled Dream while Foxy stamped her hind foot. Abigail jumped and grabbed for the saddle horn. "Just a fly. Just a fly," she whispered.

Jake laughed and rode around Dream to the other side of Abigail. He leaned over and put his hand on the front of Abigail's saddle. "If you hold on to that horn any tighter, you'll get cramps in your fingers. You'll be fine. Let go."

Abigail shook her head. "No way."

"Aaab-i-gail." He stretched out each syllable and looked sternly at her hand.

Finger-by-finger, she released it.

"Good. Now relax. Pretend you're lying on the couch watching TV."

Abigail's hand hovered near the horn. "What am I watching? *America's Funniest Home Videos* or a scary movie?"

Jake laughed again, and the dimple appeared in his cheek.

Miya looked down at her saddle. "You're watching a brand-new movie about three friends. The hero would rather be at home getting on practice calves, and the star of the show would rather be on her computer solving math equations, but they banded together to help the third friend, one who really appreciates it but doesn't deserve it," Miya said.

"Sure, you do." Jake took off his hat and scratched his head.

"Yeah, you do," Abigail said. "Even if my life ends in the next few minutes, you deserve it." Abigail held her hand over her heart for an instant before she grabbed the horn again.

At that moment, Lisa rode up, still smiling. "It's wonderful to be on horseback again. I feel ten years younger. So, my friends, let's talk about goals."

Miya piped up. "'Goals.' Jake's favorite word."

Lisa shifted on Sprint. "Alright. Let's start with Jake. What are your goals for these lessons?"

Jake grinned. "I want to be a better team with Hawk. I want to be consistent."

"'Consistent' is my favorite word. Watching you ride, I see that you have a lot of natural ability. Let's refine those skills." She turned to Abigail. "Abby, how about you?"

"I want to ride with Miya and Jake for fun. But it's not fun if I'm always worried about falling off." Foxy stretched out her neck and shook. Abigail tightened her grip on the saddle horn. "See what I mean?"

"I know," Lisa said. "We'll work on building your confidence."

Miya smiled at Abigail. "I'll help you. You'll be chasing cows in no time."

"Yeah," said Jake. "Miya and I will be saying, 'Wait up, Abigail, you're going too fast.'"

Abigail giggled and rested her hand on the swells of the saddle. Close to, but not on the saddle horn.

"Miya, what are your goals?" Miya reached forward and patted Dream's neck, too embarrassed to meet Lisa's eye. "Like I told you before, I want to be the kind of rider Dream deserves."

The breeze rustled the sagebrush. Brown sparrows darted in and out of the barn, beaks filled with dry grass and twigs. Miya stared at the black spot on Dream's neck. She felt lighter, like springtime. Lisa and her friends were giving her a chance to learn, to grow, and to begin something new.

Lisa's voice interrupted her thoughts. "Those are all good goals. Gather 'round. To start, you will learn to control all six of your horse's body parts. Head, neck, and poll." Lisa pointed to the spot right behind Sprint's ears. "The poll is the joint where the head attaches to the neck. Remember where it is because it's important. The other parts are the shoulders, ribs, and hindquarters."

Miya nodded. If she had controlled Dream better at the last race, she could have moved her away and missed the barrel. Instead, she smacked right into it.

Head. Neck. Poll. Ribs. Shoulders. Hindquarters.

Lisa rode Sprint out to a circle marked with cones. She showed them how to position their hands and feet and how to ask for the correct "arc" or bend in their horses. Miya watched Lisa in awe. She sat perfectly balanced in her saddle, her back erect, and the reins loose in her hands.

"I'd love to be able to ride like that," she whispered.

Jake swatted a horsefly that had landed on Hawk's neck. "Keep practicing and you will."

"I'd love to ride and not fall off," Abigail whispered.

"Keep practicing and you will," Jake and Miya answered together. All three laughed.

Chapter Twenty-Three

Monday, Miya covered a gigantic yawn with her hand. She'd gotten up early and had Dream saddled by 5:00 a.m. She'd spent an hour riding Dream in the arena to practice the skills Lisa taught them on Saturday. Miya would ride Dream again after school. This time she'd ride outside of the arena in the fields for fun. Riding along the trails and through the pastures would keep Dream in tip-top shape and not have her get bored or sour.

During lunch period, Miya stepped into the art room and automatically looked toward the pool of sunlight streaming through the big window. It illuminated the still-lifes, weaving, and batiks. She couldn't wait to set the sculpture of Dream in the middle of it and take a picture. She imagined Dream stretched out and running toward the edge of the light. But first, she and Mr. O had to be the veterinarians.

Over the weekend, Miya had watched several videos, taken notes, and combined the best advice from all the sculptors into a list of steps.

Miya hadn't had time to pack a real lunch, so she'd thrown string cheese, little containers of chocolate pudding, and a couple of oranges into her backpack. She thought Abigail would be okay with it. Abigail wasn't picky, except for the "tuna" thing. Leaving the food untouched, Miya headed toward Mr. O.

Mr. O looked at Ty's drawing of Mr. O in huge, pointed cowboy boots and a ten-gallon hat and a paint smock instead of a western shirt. In the sketch, Mr. O stood at an easel holding a paintbrush in one hand and a guitar in the other. Ty's pictures were all funny like that, but he hardly ever smiled.

Miya walked over and waited a little distance away. Mr. O looked up and smiled. "Miya, I found some liquid polymer for an adhesive. While I'm finishing with Ty, why don't you go over to the cupboard and find a small drill and sander with a sanding ball."

"Okay, I'll go look." As she turned to go, Tyler offered her one of his rare smiles. Miya smiled back.

Miya opened the door to the clay cupboard and rummaged around for the supplies. She set them on her table and retrieved the box that held Dream. She put it on the table and stared down at the sculpture.

Miya whispered, "I hope we can fix you."

The sound of Abigail's slapping shoes stopped beside her. Miya looked up. Abigail held up a brown lunch bag. "I brought some chocolate chip cookies in honor of your rebuilding Dream." Abigail peered down at the broken sculpture through her wire-rimmed glasses. "You can do it. I know you can."

"Thanks for the vote of confidence and the cookies." She took one and ate it while she waited for Mr. O.

When Mr. O finished talking to Ty, Miya showed him her list of steps. "Looks like you've done your homework. I'll leave you to it. Call me if you need any help." Mr. O left to help a girl at the potter's wheel.

Miya used the sanding ball to gently smooth the surfaces of both sides of the front leg. After she sanded it, she added a patch of clay to reattach it to the rest of the statue. She followed the same pattern and reconnected the rest of the parts. The sculpture would bake overnight.

Abigail tapped Miya's back. "It's time to go. I already cleaned up the lunch stuff."

"Mm-hmm." Miya tilted her head and looked at Dream. She reached for the drill again.

Abigail grabbed it and started winding up the cord.

"Hey," Miya protested.

"I know you're into this, but the coach will be furious if you're late again."

Abigail put the drill in the cupboard and threw her backpack over her shoulder. "See you later." Abigail stepped out into the hallway, and the door swung shut behind her.

As Miya gently set Dream back onto the shelf, she realized she didn't hate running anymore. She didn't love it, but these days she hardly ever came in last.

Miya headed straight to her gym locker. All the other girls were already out on the track, and the only noise she could hear was the constant running of a broken toilet. Miya smiled as she twirled the combination lock. Only a few more hours of school today, and she'd be free to ride Dream.

She felt as much as heard someone slip up behind her. Miya dropped the lock and spun around. Skylar leaned against a set of pink lockers, smiling like she had a wonderful secret.

Skylar inched forward and spoke in a voice as sweet as wild raspberries. "So, Miya, I know that you and Lily can't stand each other. Maybe you'd like to play a little joke on her."

"No thanks." The words came out short and tight.

Skylar studied the silver sparkles on her purple nails. "Come on, we're not going to hurt her or anything. All you need to do is take a video and post it. Don't you think it would be fun to get back at her for that video she shot of you?"

Miya turned back to her locker.

Behind her, Skylar continued, her voice smooth as honey. "This is what we're going to do. You know how Lily always grabs one of the private showers and gets dressed in there? I don't know why. Anyway, we'll wait until after she's dressed. Ella and I'll fill up a mop bucket from the janitor's closet, and when Lily is dressed, we'll dump it over the top of the shower curtain."

Pink paint flaked off the locker. The smell of mildew, sweaty clothes, and Skylar's kiwi-mango perfume surrounded Miya, making it difficult to breathe.

Skylar nudged Miya. "When we get the bucket in position, you open the curtain and start the video. The look on her face will be hilarious. You can post it, and we'll see if it gets as many hits as yours did."

Miya didn't say a word.

It might be great to give Lily a taste of her own medicine and let her see what it feels like to be made fun of and hurt so bad that she won't want to get out of bed.

"You know she wants Jake. This will teach her not to mess with you."

Jake's name made up Miya's mind. She turned and faced Skylar. "All I have to do is video?"

"That's all." Skylar smiled. "We'll take care of the rest."

"Okay."

"Good. Paybacks are great, you'll see."

Skylar's gym shoes squeaked as she retreated. Miya pulled on her gym clothes and jogged out the door.

Coach stood with both hands on her hips as Miya ran toward the field. Her tanned, wrinkled legs stuck out from under khaki shorts. "Don't bother with your laps, Miya. Just find your place. You'll run doubles tomorrow."

Miya found her place and started stretching. She needed to talk to the coach without the others listening in, but how?

"Burpee time!" Coach yelled.

The kids groaned, but most of them slowly dropped to a plank position. Miya hated burpees because they made her fat jiggle. Today though, they gave her an idea. Miya struggled through four burpees while she gathered up her nerve. She hated being the center of attention, having all the kids stare at her, but she couldn't think of any other option. Miya threw her legs out and started rolling on the ground, screaming, "My ankle, my ankle!"

Coach ran over, and the kids gathered in a loose circle around her. Miya saw the flash of the sun reflected off a screen.

Seriously? They managed to video her even when phones were banned in PE?

"What happened?" Coach said, kneeling next to Miya. "Where are you hurt?"

"It's my ankle." Miya let her voice quaver. Coach reached for Miya's foot. "No, don't touch it!" Miya screamed and pulled her foot closer to her. "Just help me over to the bench."

Coach signaled for two of the girls to help her.

"No, No!" Miya tried to sound hysterical. "I just want *you* to help me."

"Choose up teams and play kickball. I'll be back in a minute."

Miya put her arm around coach's shoulders and pretended to limp. As soon as they were out of earshot, Miya said, "I didn't really hurt my ankle. I needed to talk to you alone before the end of the period."

Coach straightened and tried to face Miya. Miya hung on more tightly around Coach's neck. "Please, please. Just listen. The reason I'm so late is because Skylar Peters caught me in the locker room. She and Ella are going to wait until Lily gets dressed and then dump a bucket full of cold water over her. They want me to video it."

Miya and Coach continued walking. "Miya, this is a serious accusation." Coach frowned. "Skylar and Ella are such nice girls. I don't believe they would do anything like this. But if it will make you feel better, we'll call them over and get to the bottom of this."

Miya shook her head in frustration. "No. If we warn them, they'll know I ratted them out, and they'll just be sneakier next time."

Coach looked doubtful. When they reached the bench, Miya sat down, holding her leg out in front of her. "Could you just wait until after class? Skylar and Ella are counting on you going to your office. Instead, wait behind the second group of lockers. When you see them getting the bucket in place, you can catch them in the act." Miya could video Skylar and Ella as proof.

"I honestly don't know if I can believe you, Miya. You don't like PE, and you're always late for class. Skylar and Ella, on the other hand, are two of my best athletes."

Disappointed, Miya couldn't meet the coach's eye. "Today, they're not out for me. They want Lily. I'm just trying to stand up and do the right thing."

Coach sighed. "Since you're already here, you can continue this charade for today. I'll think about what you told me."

Miya watched the coach stride back toward the game. Skylar just made a home run, and her teammates jumped up and down and congratulated her. Lily, who played second base on the other team, ran all the way across the field to hug Skylar.

Miya sighed and put her "injured" ankle up on the bench. She wished Emily from math class were here. Emily would have helped, but she was on a trip to Washington D.C. She'd written an essay on leadership and won first place.

Miya ran her fingers along the edge of the bench. She'd tried to speak up, stand up, and do the right thing. If the grownups wouldn't believe her, it was out of her hands. She'd get dressed and leave the locker room. At least there wouldn't be a video to post, unlike Lily's video of her barrel race.

Miya's shoulders drooped, feeling like they weighed about a million pounds. Jake. If he found out she'd walked away, he'd be so disappointed in her. She thought about everyone else: Lisa, Abigail, Mom and Dad, Mr. O. None of them would take the easy, safe option and slink away. If she somehow managed to save Lily, Skylar and Ella and their group would make life miserable for her for the rest of the year, probably through high school, too.

The teams changed sides. Skylar claimed the pitcher's mound, and Ella pranced out to first base. Coach blew the whistle, and Lily, the first kicker, stepped up to home plate.

Miya didn't know how many more times she could hide in her bed while her heart broke. The rotten part was, even if she stood up to Skylar's group, Lily probably wouldn't even appreciate it.

When the period was almost over, the class gathered up orange plastic bases and headed toward the locker room. Ella dribbled the ball over to Miya and leaned in close. "Can you still video?"

How did Ella even know Miya had agreed? They probably took for granted that she would. Everyone did what the popular kids wanted.

"Uh, yeah," Miya said, keeping her eyes on her ankle.

"Good. It will be so funny." Ella smiled and dribbled the ball to the locker room.

After waiting for everyone else to go inside, Miya heaved herself off the bench and walked inside. Once there, she fake-limped over to her locker. She dressed quickly and got out her phone as Lily disappeared behind the shower curtain. Coach closed her office door behind her. Skylar and Ella dragged the bucket toward the shower next to Lily's stall. Though her legs felt like they were made of cement blocks, Miya limped to the front of Lily's stall. She clutched her phone as she watched Skylar climb on the bench and Ella hand the bucket to her.

Giggles spread across the locker room. Anticipation mounted like the night before a big concert.

Skylar pointed to Miya. "Ready?" she whispered.

Miya nodded. She wished she could get the right angle to video Skylar and Ella, but they were hidden behind the shower stall wall. Time to put Plan B into effect. She figured she had about five seconds until the two girls hoisted the bucket to the top of the wall.

She jerked the curtain back and shouted, "Lily, move!" Her voice echoed through the locker room.

Lily looked at her in surprise; shock froze her in place. Miya saw the rim of the bucket appear over the top of the shower. Out of time, she jumped forward and pushed Lily out of the way just as the bucket tipped, and five gallons of soapy mop-bucket water splashed on top of Miya's head.

Miya coughed and sputtered. The bucket clattered to the floor. Miya reached up and picked a gray-white mop string out of her hair. Her shirt sagged around her shoulders. Her jeans felt like they weighed a hundred pounds. She looked down at her hand, still clutching her phone. Like her, it had been soaked.

Miya sighed, imagining the videos the other girls were taking. Drowned rat Mega Miya. She looked at Lily scrunched up against the side of the shower. Lily's jeans and sandals had been splashed, but at least she wasn't drenched.

Lily's mouth formed a round "O." She looked from her wet sandals to Miya's drenched clothes. Her breath caught in a small sob.

Skylar and Ella appeared in front of the stall. Their mirrored looks of amazement reminded Miya of a couple of hens who'd just laid their first eggs.

"I am so disappointed in you both," said Coach, her voice sharp. Her eyes narrowed at Skylar and Ella. "I saw the whole thing. The three of us are going to the office where it will be my mission to make sure you are dealt with properly." She glanced at Miya as she passed. "Miya, call your mother and ask her to bring you some dry clothes."

Miya nodded and looked down at her dripping phone. How? Her phone was as wet as she was.

Skylar started to sputter. "Coach, it's not what it looks like. Miya and Lily are such good friends of ours that we were playing a little prank to have some fun. Ella thought it up. . . ."

Ella shot Skylar a poisonous look. "I did not! You . . ."

Coach held up her hand. "I have a question. How did you think you would get away with this?"

Skylar giggled and shrugged. "It was really just a little joke. We were going to pour a tiny drop of water on Lily's head. Not enough that anyone would notice. Ella slipped and poured too much . . ."

"I did not!" Ella stamped her foot.

"Save it for the principal," Coach said. "Let's go."

One by one, the rest of the girls followed the coach, Skylar, and Ella out of the locker room until only Miya and Lily remained.

Miya rung out the hem of her soaking new shirt. Miya's stomach shook like she just got off the Tilt-A-Whirl at the fair. She sat down on the bench.

Lily sat down beside her. "I can't believe Skylar and Ella did that. Were they really trying to get me or you?"

"You. Skylar told me about the plan before PE. They wanted me to video it." Miya squeezed mucky, soapy water out of her braid.

"Oh." Lily deflated a little. "I thought they were my friends."

"I know you did." Miya stared down at the suds in the drain. "You can still be my friend."

Lily looked at Miya. "Maybe. I still can't believe Skylar and Ella would do this to me. I did everything they wanted."

Miya touched her arm. "Don't you think it's better you found out about them now rather than after something bigger happens?"

When Lily didn't respond, Miya stood up. "Listen. I need to take a shower and change back into my P.E. clothes. Will you call my mom?"

"Sure." Lily scrolled through her phone.

Miya's shoes sloshed down the aisle to her locker, and she gathered her clothes and shampoo. She squelched back to the shower and turned on the water as hot as she could stand it. Miya squirted a big glob of white shampoo into her hand and began working it through her hair.

While rubbing her scalp with her fingertips, Miya pictured Lily, now safe and dry. Then, Miya recalled the way Skylar's and Ella's eyes had bugged out. Miya giggled. She'd done it. She, Miya Skippingbird, had stepped up. Smiling to herself, Miya reached for a towel.

"No, Mrs. Skippingbird, she's not hurt. She got wet when water fell on the top of her head." Miya peeked out from the shower. Lily had her ear pressed to her phone. "It's kind of hard to explain how a bucket of water fell on her. . . ." Lily's voice trailed off, and she held the phone away from her ear.

Miya heard Mom's voice on the other end of the line. She couldn't make out the words, but Mom did not sound happy.

After a few seconds, Lily cautiously brought the phone back to her ear. "Can you bring some dry clothes for Miya and meet us at the principal's office?" She waited. After a few seconds, Lily said, "Goodbye, Mrs. Skippingbird. See you soon."

Miya stuffed her wet clothes into her gym bag. She hoped her new shirt wasn't ruined forever. "Ready?" she asked Lily.

"Yep." Lily slipped her phone into her back pocket. "We'd better get to the office before your mom comes looking for you to make sure you're really okay."

"Good idea." Miya held the door for Lily. The two walked toward the office.

Miya's thoughts tumbled around and around, like the rocks in the polisher she had gotten one year for Christmas. Miya was still mad at Lily, but she felt a little bit sorry for her at the same time. Miya didn't know what to say, so she studied the posters that lined the hallway. She thought that the student council had gone a little overboard with their glitter pens to advertise the spring dance.

As Miya and Lily entered the office, Mrs. Bates, the school secretary, looked over her glasses at them and nodded toward two chairs. Miya sat down and set the gym bag containing her wet clothes at her feet.

Lily threw herself into the other chair and chewed on her thumbnail. "I still can't believe they did that to me."

Before Miya could answer, she heard the *CLICK-CLICK-CLICK* of her mother's heels marching down the hall. Mom was only a little over five feet tall, but she reminded Miya of an angry grizzly bear as she burst through the door. Miya had once seen a sow grizzly chase down a coyote who had gotten too close to her cub. Miya thought her mom had that same look in her eye. Mom's gaze locked on the two girls. "Honey, are you and Lily all right?"

Miya stood up and hugged Mom. "Yes, Mom, we're fine. Please, don't embarrass me."

"Oh, I don't intend to embarrass you. I intend to see something gets done. I see Skylar and Ella and their parents are in Mr. Dustlyn's office. I'm going to step in there and make sure that they are aware of the bullying going on. Now is the time to put an end to it."

She swept into the office. Miya saw Mr. Dustlyn jump to his feet. He held out his hand, and Mom shook it with a quick up and down motion. The principal gestured toward a chair, but Mom shook her head and turned to the other parents. By the way she stood, Miya thought Mom had really channeled her inner grizzly. Mr. Dustlyn talked. Coach stood with him behind his desk. Skylar's and Ella's parents sat stiffly on the edges of their chairs while their daughters slouched low.

"Wow, it looks like your mom is ready to bite someone's head off," Lily said.

Miya shifted on the hard seat. "I know, right? The other parents look pretty mad, too."

Mr. Dustlyn turned the monitor so the group could see the video of what had happened in the locker room. Mom finally sat down. When the video was over, the coach started talking. Skylar's mom said something, but Coach shook her head.

Mr. Dustlyn started the video again. Mom jumped to her feet, pointed to something on the screen, and then faced Skylar's mom with her hands on her hips.

"I'd say your mom has your back," said Lily.

Warmth, like a cup of hot chocolate, spread through Miya's veins. It didn't seem to matter that Skylar's and Ella's moms had nicer clothes and better hair. Mom wasn't afraid to stand up for Miya.

"Yeah, I think she does."

Finally, Mom shook Mr. Dustlyn's hand, nodded to the other parents, and with her head held high, walked out the door.

"Come on, Miya, let's go home. Mr. Dustlyn will make sure that you get excused absences for your last two classes. Lily, would you like a ride home, too?"

"No thanks," Lily said, looking at the carpet. "I'll just go back to class." She tugged the door open just wide enough to slip through and disappear into the hallway.

Silently, Miya and Mom walked out to the parking lot. The sunshine felt warm on Miya's back. The clouds floated in the endless blue sky. Miya waited until they had buckled their seatbelts before she turned to Mom. "What went on in Mr. Dustlyn's office?"

Mom started the car but didn't put it in reverse. "Skylar's and Ella's parents tried to defend their daughters, but there wasn't much they could say. Your coach got ahold of a phone of one of the girls who videoed the whole thing. She sent it to Mr. Dustlyn so the evidence was there for all to see. Mr. Dustlyn assured me that there will be consequences. Better yet, it made him aware of what is going on in the hallways and locker rooms of his school."

"And the cafeteria. That's where a lot of the bullying happens."

Mom squeezed her hand. "The cafeteria, too? Why didn't you tell me about it before? I would have talked to Mr. Dustlyn sooner."

"I don't know." Miya stared out the windshield. "I guess I just accepted it. Most of the time it's not horrible, but there comes the point when you have to stand up." She smiled at Mom. "Thanks for standing up with me."

Mom smiled back. "I'm proud of you, sweetheart. I'll stand with you anytime. That's what I'm here for." She put the car in gear, and Miya and Mom started home.

Chapter Twenty-Four

Miya brushed Dream's neck, back, sides, and legs. The evening sun slanted inside the barn door where Zoey lay, dozing on an old horse blanket in a bed of straw and snoring softly. Occasionally, her legs twitched as though she were chasing a rabbit.

Dream's ears flicked forward, and she nickered. Zoey jumped up and barked.

CLIP-CLOP. CLIP-CLOP. Miya heard hoofbeats on the hard-packed dirt of the barnyard.

Miya reached over the stall door and slid the bolt back. "Just a minute, girl," she said to Dream. "It sounds like someone's here."

With Zoey at her heels, Miya walked to the barn door. Lily slid off her horse, Poco.

"Hey," Lily said, concentrating a little too hard on tying the knot to the hitching rail. "I haven't ridden Poco in so long, and I couldn't concentrate on my homework, so . . ." Lily shrugged. "I decided to ride over here."

"Cool." Miya stood awkwardly in the barn door for a few moments. "Come on in. I'm brushing Dream." She went into Dream's stall. Lily followed a few feet behind. Zoey walked over to Lily and nudged her hand.

Lily dropped to her knees and smoothed back Zoey's ears. Still staring into Zoey's deep brown eyes, she spoke. "So," Lily drew the word out, "I really came to talk to you about what you did today. I thought a lot about it, and I realized Skylar was using me all this time. I didn't deserve your help, but thanks."

Miya concentrated on brushing a black spot on Dream's back. She didn't look up. "Welcome." She gathered her courage. "I know I told you this before, but you really hurt me."

"I hurt you?" Lily stood up and stepped closer to the stall. "What about what you did? As soon as the new girl moved in, you ditched me without a word. You wouldn't even answer my texts. Then, you wouldn't even look at me or talk to me, at lunch, at the jackpot, at PE. You left me just like my dad did."

Tears clung to the ends of Lily's lashes. Her hands were balled into fists. Miya shivered as the words seemed to swirl around her.

You left me just like my dad did.

Miya swallowed. "Sorry." The word came out in a whisper. Miya cleared her throat and tried again. "I'm sorry I ditched you. It's just that you've been so mad at everyone lately, I thought you'd be mean to Abigail like all the other kids."

"I know." Lily sighed and leaned over the stall door.

Dream walked over to Lily and blew gently on her face. Lily rubbed Dream's forehead.

Miya remembered how she didn't want to get out of bed after all the horrible posts online. She remembered how the cruel comments had piled up, crushing her under their weight.

Miya looked at Lily. "Did you have to do all that mean stuff?"

"No," Lily whispered, more to Dream than to Miya.

Miya waited for Lily to apologize. And waited. She held the brush so tightly that the edge made a print in her palm. Lily didn't speak. She didn't look at Miya.

Dad appeared in the doorway. "Hi, girls."

Miya looked at him. His sleeves were rolled part-way up on his tanned forearms, his straw hat pushed back on his head.

201

"Hey, Dad." Miya sighed and turned to Lily. "I'm glad you rode Poco over. Lisa's been giving us riding lessons on Saturday mornings. I bet she wouldn't mind if you came, too."

Lily glanced at Miya. "Poco doesn't have any shoes."

Dad moved to the stall door. He smiled at Lily. "Why don't you bring Poco over in a couple days, and I'll tack some shoes on him?"

Lily looked from Dad to Miya. "I'll see if Mom is off Saturday morning and can watch the kids. I'll come if I can."

She went to the door and turned back. "Thanks again, Miya."

"You're welcome."

Miya and Dad walked with Lily to the hitching rail where Lily untied an old, baggy sweatshirt from the back of her saddle and slipped it on. The front pocket was torn part-way off. Miya liked that it made Lily look more like herself before she started trying to impress everyone.

Lily climbed into the saddle and turned Poco toward her home. She looked over her shoulder and waved. Miya and Dad waved back. They watched until Poco and his rider disappeared from sight.

"Your mom told me the whole story about what happened at school today." Dad hugged Miya. "I'm pretty proud of you, Miya-girl."

Dad smelled good, like hay and horse feed. "Thanks. It was nice that Lily came over to thank me, but I wish that she had apologized for all the stuff she did."

Dad let Miya go and reached down to pet Zoey. He picked a burr out of the long hair under Zoey's front legs. "Lily's lost so much. She's still upset. Thanking you is enough for now."

"Every time I think about what Lily did to me, I get mad, and I'm tired of being mad. It's hard to forgive Lily when she won't admit that she's done anything wrong."

Dad pulled her into another hug. "Most of the time we forgive for our own peace of mind, not for others'. I'm not saying what she did was okay but try to forgive her. Every time you get mad about it, try to forgive her again. Eventually, you'll feel better."

Miya leaned against him a minute longer. "I'll do my best." She sighed. "I never thought growing up would be so hard."

Dad reached over and picked a piece of alfalfa out of Miya's hair. He opened his fingers, and the tiny purple flowers drifted to the ground. "I know, but you're doing a good job of it." He stepped toward the barn. "Let's get the rest of these horses fed and go eat. I'm starving."

* * *

Miya sat on the bus beside Jake. She cradled the completed sculpture of Dream in her lap. It wasn't perfect. One back leg was a little crooked. One ear didn't quite match the other. That was okay. It had taken a lot of time and effort to rebuild Dream. She'd almost given up a few times. With Mr. O's and Abigail's encouragement, she worked through it. Now she held something she was proud of.

There were only two days left of school, and she couldn't wait to ride Dream along the creek this summer.

"How did you do on your math final?"

"I got an 89%. B-plus." She smiled across the aisle at Abigail. "Because of Abigail, I'm starting to get math."

Lily and Abigail sat together and shared a bag of chips. Abigail finished chewing and smiled back. "I might have

203

helped you with math, but you helped Mr. Callahan. Next year, I'll bet he'll do better at teaching all the kids, not just the smart ones."

Lily crumpled up the empty chip bag and put it in her backpack. She hadn't worn eyeliner or mascara for the past week. She wore a gray T-shirt under a maroon, zip-up hoodie instead of her usual low-cut tank top.

"Abigail," Lily said. "Didn't you go to the math team meeting yesterday? How was it?"

"Fine. I like math challenges. A few of the kids were kind of stuck up, but the others were nice. The math team gets together during lunch in high school. Maybe I'll join them sometimes."

"What?" Miya pretended to gasp and fall back in her seat. "You won't be perfecting your landscapes? What will I do without you? I hope to hang out in the art room again. I have an idea for a sculpture that includes beadwork and tooled leather."

Lily said, "Maybe I'll hang out with you while Abigail goes to math club."

"You can if you want, Lily."

"I signed you up, Miya," Jake said, turning from the bus window.

Miya looked up from the sculpture. "Signed me up for what?"

"This week's jackpot. Lisa says you're ready to compete again. Maybe not win . . . but you'll make a smooth run."

"What were you thinking? I'm not running. I haven't even looked at a barrel since that last disaster."

Jake nodded. "That's the point. All the drills we've been doing have helped build the foundation you need. Lisa said with all the extra riding you've been doing on your own, you're ready."

Miya shook her head. No way this fat girl would make a fool of herself again.

Jake threw his arm around Miya's shoulder and squeezed her. "C'mon. I'll be riding a bull. You cheer for me, I'll cheer for you. Besides, Dream deserves a second chance. This time, we'll post a video you're proud of."

Miya stared at Jake for a long moment. His dimple appeared along with his killer smile. After squeezing Miya's shoulder one more time, he released it and put his arm back in his lap. He waited a beat and then wiggled his eyebrows up and down. "Say yes, Miya."

Miya laughed as Jake wiggled his eyebrows. It worked every time. When her giggles faded away, she looked down at the Dream sculpture again. Maybe she should step up for Dream.

Miya blew out her breath. "Okay, yes."

Jake grinned even bigger and squeezed her hand.

Chapter Twenty-Five

At Saturday's jackpot, mini bull riding came before barrel racing. Miya figured she had enough time to watch Jake ride before she had to warm up Dream. Lily sat beside Miya in the stands. Noah and Paislee were seated on each side of Mom, eating cotton candy. Both of them had bright blue lips and tongues. Miya jiggled her boot, waiting for Jake's name to be called.

Lily leaned over and said in a muffled voice, "You can have Jake. He's hot, but I know he's into you. I was only going after him to get back at you."

Miya blushed. "I don't think he likes me, you know, as anything more than a friend."

Lily rolled her eyes. "Are you blind? Of course, he likes you. Everybody knows it."

"Shhhh!" Miya said and nodded toward Mom while turning bright red. "My mom or Jake's might hear you. That would be so embarrassing."

Miya turned back toward the arena, but not before she saw Mom wink at Janelle. She blushed again—all the way to the tips of her ears.

Just then, the chute gate opened, and Jake's bull jumped into the arena.

The bell on the bull rope *CLANG-CLANGED-CLANGED*. The black bull twisted. The red fringe on Jake's chaps whipped. Miya held her breath. She clenched her hand around an imaginary bull rope.

Lily cheered. "Hustle, Jake, hustle!"

Paislee clapped her chubby hands. "Go, Jakie, go!"

The horn sounded with an echoing *WAAAAAH*. Jake jumped off and landed in the dirt. He ran to the arena fence and jumped on it as the bull loped by. Underneath his helmet, Miya knew he was laughing. He'd stayed on his first bull of the season.

Lily stamped her feet. Paislee kept clapping. Noah grinned a big blue grin and stuffed the rest of the cotton candy into his mouth.

"What a wonderful ride!" said Mom. "Jake had great control until the very end."

"Yeah, and it was a quick little bull," said Jake's mom.

The speakers crackled. "Ladies and gentlemen, we have a score for Jake Runningdeer." Miya held her breath. The announcer cleared his throat. "We have a score of 78 for that cowboy. Nice job, Jake."

Miya and Lily high-fived. The moms cheered. A 78 might not be the winning score for the day, but Jake had ridden well.

Miya stood up. Her legs shook, and she couldn't swallow. Her voice came out as a hoarse croak. "I'm gonna get Dream and start warming her up."

Mom stood up and gave Miya a hug. "Dream and you will both do great. I know it."

"Jake told me you were stressed about the first barrel," said Jake's mom. "Don't worry about it. You've got this."

"Yeah, Miya!" Noah and Paislee clapped their sticky hands. "You got this," yelled Noah.

Paislee's tiny voice echoed Noah's, "You got this!"

Lily stood up beside Miya. She held up her phone. "I'll ask you if it's okay before I post the video today. I have a feeling that people are going to start calling you Flying Miya."

Flying Miya? Miya smiled as she walked down the bleachers. Miya didn't care if she flew, she just wanted to make a good clean run. She didn't want to embarrass herself or let Dream down.

As Miya crossed the parking lot, her thoughts turned to Jake's ride. She was proud of him. She'd buy him some nachos to celebrate. If Miya managed to stay calm and apply what she'd learned from Lisa, she'd celebrate by buying herself some nachos, too.

When Miya arrived at the horse trailer, she found Lisa leaning on her cane and petting Dream. Abigail sat on Foxy, clutching the saddle horn. Miya looked at Abigail in surprise. "You're riding Foxy in public? I thought you were only comfortable at home."

"I am. Grandma said it would take your mind off your nerves if I warmed up with you." She frowned at Lisa. "I told her I could be a supportive friend without endangering my life, but she said, 'Cowgirl up, Abby.' What do you think of that?"

"I think you're the best. You, too, Lisa."

"Well, thank you," said Lisa. "You will be fine, Abby. It's time to get outside your comfort zone a bit. Foxy's been to a hundred jackpots and has seen it all. She will take care of you."

Abigail let the reins slide through her fingers. She patted Foxy's neck. "Please, faithful steed, do not dump me in a mud puddle."

After Miya mounted, Lisa slipped the rubber bands on her feet and patted Miya's knee. "Concentrate on being smooth and have fun. That's what this is really all about."

Lisa turned and hobbled toward the stands.

Miya and Abigail walked the horses around in circles behind the alley. Miya couldn't help but look at the other barrel racers. They looked just as confident as they did the last time Miya ran, just as together.

Abigail chattered about a stray cat having kittens in their barn yesterday. Miya had already heard the story, but she listened anyway. It kept her mind off throwing up.

Miya took a mental inventory. She wore her good luck jeans, had rubber bands on her boots, and had her hat tightly pulled down over her braid. She laid her reins on Dream's neck and wiped her palms on her jeans.

"Miya!"

She looked up at the contestant stand where Jake balanced on the very end of the very top bleacher. He flashed her a thumbs up. "Good luck!"

She returned the thumbs up.

"Miya Skippingbird," the speakers called. "Be getting it on your mind."

Miya counted to six as she and Abigail moved closer to the end of the alley where Dad waited. Abigail stopped Foxy where she had a good view of the arena. "Go get 'em, Miya!"

Dad smiled at her when she rode up to him. He rechecked her cinch and rubber bands, unwrapped a chocolate bar and gave half to Dream. "You get the other half if you run fast," he told the horse with a pat.

"Miya Skippingbird, you're up."

Dad smiled and tapped her stirrup twice. "Proud of you, Miya-girl. Have fun."

"Yeah, have fun!" Abigail called and waved before she grabbed the saddle horn again.

Miya smiled. She guided Dream into the alley and leaned slightly forward in the saddle, signaling Dream to trot, not lope. The last time they'd run the entire length of the alley, and Dream was tired by the time they'd reached the first barrel. Miya wouldn't make that mistake again. Toward the end of the alley, Miya squeezed her legs, asking Dream to lope, and by the time they passed the electric eye, they were at a gallop. The official run had begun. Miya and Dream were not running flat out yet but were galloping with control.

Miya's heart beat hard as she reached the first barrel. She transferred her weight back in the saddle, asking Dream to rate, or turn at the correct spot. Dream responded, and she rounded it in a flash. Miya couldn't believe it. They had made a nice turn around the dreaded first barrel!

Miya leaned forward, encouraging Dream to run hard for the second barrel. They made a smooth turn around the second barrel and headed toward the third. Miya concentrated on her pocket, or the spot she wanted Dream to run to, but Dream drifted in toward the third barrel. When they were six strides away, Miya realized they were going to hit it, just like the last time.

"No," Miya whispered. "Not a five-second penalty!" She almost jerked on the reins in her panic, but then she remembered what Lisa had taught her—move Dream over by using leg cues. They were getting closer to the barrel! She kicked Dream lightly with her right leg.

Move over, girl! Move over!

Dream still headed straight toward the barrel. Miya didn't give up.

KICK. KICK.

Dream widened her arc, missing the barrel, and turned it perfectly. She sprinted toward home and Foxy.

"18.79 for Miya Skippingbird," the announcer said as Miya waited at the gate to leave the arena.

18.79. Miya couldn't believe her ears. Miya leaned forward and hugged Dream.

Miya's family, Jake's family, Lisa and Abigail, and Lily and her siblings met at the trailer. Miya unsaddled Dream while hugging and high-fiving everyone. Lisa got a can of pop out of the cooler, and balancing herself on her cane with one hand, held up the drink with the other. "I'd like to propose a toast to two hard-working kids. To Jake who covered his first bull of the season and to Miya who worked with her horse and made a beautiful, smooth run."

Miya smiled. "Thanks, Lisa, for all the coaching. And thanks, Mom and Dad."

Abigail took a gulp of her grandma's pop and held it up. "I'd like to propose a toast to me, who was scared to death on Foxy today, and to Lily, who's now our friend."

Lily shrugged but pulled her brother and sister closer into the group gathered at the trailer.

After Dream had been watered and covered with a light sheet, Jake walked around the pickup eating a ham sandwich. He wiped the mustard off his chin with the back of his arm. "Hey guys, want to go over and check the standings? They should be posted by now."

"I'll watch the little ones," said Mom. "You kids go over."

"I don't think I want to," Miya said. "I made a good run, but I know I wasn't fast enough to win."

Jake grabbed Miya's hand and started tugging on it. "Because seeing the winning time will give you something to strive for, and we can sign up for the next jackpot while we're there."

"But I can do that online later." She'd only heard a couple of the other times, and both runs were faster than hers. Miya hoped that she had finished in the top half.

"I think Jake's right," said Abigail. "You need to do this. We'll be right there with you. Grandma made me face my fears. Now, it's your turn."

After dragging her boots through the gravel, Miya stood with her friends in front of the office building with the sagging door. A fat bee buzzed around the threshold. Miya wondered if it was the same bee she'd seen the last time. A group of bull riders crowded around the list of the day's results tacked to the wall.

While Miya and her friends waited, Jake roped Lily. She laughed and tried to pull the rope out of his hands, and Abigail ran to help her. Miya stood and watched them, shifting her weight from one foot to the other. She didn't feel like playing around.

The bull riders turned to leave. A skinny kid with manure on his jeans said, "Hey, Runningdeer, good ride today."

"Thanks," Jake said as he and the girls moved up to take a look at the list. "We'll look at barrel racing first," said Jake.

"No," said Miya. "Let's check bull riding first."

"Okay. Fine," said Jake. "We'll do it your way." Heads together, the four checked the results. Lily found Jake's name first. "Whoo hoo! Jake, you're number 3. You drew a check."

"Yay, yay!" Miya said. She and Abigail hugged him.

"Okay guys, people are waiting to look at the standings. Let's check out the barrel racing," Jake said.

Miya held her breath and began to scan the page name by name, time by time. She didn't see her name. Had she been disqualified somehow?

"There you are," Abigail yelled and jumped up and down. "There you are. Miya Skippingbird. 18.79."

"Where? Where does it say that?" Miya frantically searched the names.

"Right there. Number 9," Abigail said. She threw her arms around Miya while Jake pounded her on the back.

Lily whipped out her phone and took a picture of the results. "Miya, if it's okay with you, I'm going to post the video and your time with #flyingmiya. Skylar and Ella will just die when they see this."

Miya shook her head. "No, that feels too much like bragging. How about this? You can post the run and the time but not the hashtag part. It doesn't matter what Skylar and Ella think. I want to keep improving for my own sake, and for Dream's."

"Your run was great. You've gotten so much better since last time," said Jake. "C'mon. Let's go sign up for next time." He held the door with a grin and a bow. "After you."

"Lily and I will meet you at the horse trailer," said Abigail.

Jake and Miya walked into the small office and joined the long line of people collecting checks and signing up for the next jackpot. The rodeo secretary answered everyone's questions in a brisk, no-nonsense tone.

Miya and Jake sat down on a bench to wait. Miya laid her head back against the wall and closed her eyes. She felt as though she were still riding Dream, sprinting down the arena toward home. Miya pictured Dream's outstretched neck and flattened ears. She felt Dream's muscles bunched under the saddle. Miya's heart pounded. She thought it was the best feeling in the entire world to be part of a team with a horse that loved to run.

After a few minutes, Jake elbowed her in the side. "Come on. It's our turn."

Miya stood up and walked to the counter with him. She couldn't wait to sign up to run again.

Epilogue

Dream nibbled the apple slice that Miya held in her outstretched hand. Dream bumped Miya's hand with her nose. The apple slice fell off her palm and into the straw below. Zoey jumped up and sniffed it. Jake bent down and picked up the apple slice. "Here you go, Dream. Let's try that again."

This time, Dream got ahold of the apple and crunched it. Jake wiped the apple juice on his jeans. After they each patted Dream one more time, Jake and Miya walked to the barn door. "Sweet dreams, Dream," Miya called back.

Jake and Miya started up the path toward the house. Far away a coyote *YIP-YIP-YIPPED* and another answered back. Miya liked that nighttime sound. It reminded her of freedom and the mountains and wide-open spaces.

Jake and Miya reached the tire swing, and Miya sat down on it. She gripped the bumpy edge of frayed rubber. The light from the house glowed warm and yellow from the living room windows. Miya heard the murmur of the movie that Mom and Dad watched inside. The evening's cool air whispered over Miya's cheeks as she tilted her head back to admire the delicate sliver of a moon.

Jake grabbed the swing and twirled and twirled Miya. When he let go, Miya leaned back and watched a million stars spin by.

Just a few months ago, she had sat on this swing, trying not to cry as she felt her life unfurl. Now, she spun toward new things. High school. Art. Barrel racing. And Jake.

The brightness of the stars made Miya feel brave—even daring. "Jake, how do you feel about stuff now that the school year is over?"

Jake caught the swing and pulled it to a stop. He stood so close that Miya could have touched the smooth fabric of his down vest.

"Are you wearing cologne?"

Jake laughed. "Maybe I sprayed on a little. I didn't want to come over here smelling like sweat. Anyway, what stuff are you talking about?"

Miya inhaled again and decided she liked the smell. She shook her head and took a firmer grip on the side of the tire. "You know, stuff . . . like me and you."

Jake pushed the swing again. Around and around it sailed, dipping and spinning into the inky blackness.

"Oh, that stuff." Jake's voice was warm in the moonlight. "That stuff, I like just fine."

"You do?"

"Yep. You were always my friend, but I like how you've changed this year. You're not standing back and hiding anymore. You're . . . you're . . . I don't know."

"Stepping up?"

"Yeah, stepping up."

Miya smiled. Stepping up had been hard, but it had changed her. She kind of liked the new Miya she was becoming. Judging from Jake's laughter, he kind of liked it, too.

Study Questions

Chapters 1-2

1. What is Miya's relationship with her father? Use examples from the text to support your answer.

2. What do you think would happen if she told Dad that the kids called her "Mega Miya"?

3. What is Miya's plan for being accepted by the rodeo kids? Do you think it will work?

4. Dad says that Dragon isn't the right horse for Miya. Do you agree with him?

5. How does Miya feel about Dream? Find specific words in the passage to support your answer.

Chapters 3-4

1. Describe Jake Runningdeer. Discuss both his physical features and his personality.

2. What are Miya's feelings about math class?

3. Abigail gets bullied in the cafeteria. How does Miya feel about this? How does Lily feel?

4. Why is Miya disillusioned about the anti-bullying programs at her school?

Chapters 5-7

1. Compare and contrast the way Abigail looks and acts at school with how she looks and acts at home.

2. What is Miya's plan for lunch?

3. Describe Mr. O. Do you think he understands Miya's real reason for wanting to be in his classroom during lunch?

4. How do you think Lily is feeling in chapter 7?

5. Do you agree with Mr. O. that Miya should try an easier sculpture? Why or why not?

Chapters 8-9

1. In Chapter 8, Lisa, Abigail's grandmother says, "Don't give up on your hopes. Giving up on small ones leads to giving up on bigger ones. And life without hope is nothing." Do you agree with this? Have you ever had to give up on one of your hopes?

2. What is Jake's goal? What are some of the steps Jake is taking to achieve his goal?

Chapters 10-12

1. In your opinion, did Miya do the right thing when she didn't ask Lily to eat with her and Abigail in the art room? Why or why not?

2. How does Abigail save Miya? Do you think it was hard for Abigail to speak up to Mr. Callahan so he would switch his focus from Miya to her?

3. Why is Miya getting frustrated with her sculpture? Do you think she should make something easier now that she's tried to make a running horse?

4. How does Miya feel both before and after she rides Dream in Chapter 11?

5. How is Lily getting revenge on Miya?

6. Do you think Miya should ride Dream or Frosty when she gathers? Give reasons for your answer.

Chapters 13-14

1. How did Miya, Dream, and Jake feel about the goat?
2. Jake and Miya laugh about two childhood memories. What is a memory you have about you and a friend?
3. How do Miya's feelings about Dream change by the end of gathering day?
4. Do you think Jake gave Miya good advice on her problem with Lily? If Miya follows it do you think she and Lily will become friends again?
5. What happened to Abigail's parents?
6. How does Miya feel about the advice Lisa gives her? Do you think Miya should follow it? Why or why not?

Chapters 15-17

1. Why do you think Miya isn't willing to follow Lisa's or Jake's advice about training Dream?
2. Lily says that she didn't bully Abigail in the cafeteria. Miya says all the students did. With whom do you agree? Why?
3. The art room is described numerous times in the novel. Draw a picture of how you envision it. Include Mr. O.
4. How did Emily help Miya in PE? Do you think it took courage for Emily to help her? Why or why not?
5. How is Dream's training progressing in Chapter 16?
6. Was Jake disappointed when he didn't make a qualified ride? How would you have felt if you were Jake?

7. Jake says to Miya, "I'm tired of listening to excuses. Decide you're going to do it. You may not win the first time out; heck, you might not win the next twenty times, but you'll be a whole lot faster than you are sitting in the stands daydreaming about it." Is he being mean or helpful?

8. Miya enters up to run in the next jackpot. Do you feel she and Dream are ready? Use the text in Chapter 16 to support your answer.

Chapters 18-20

1. Is Miya willing to listen to Lisa's advice as they get closer to the jackpot?

2. Did Miya do the right thing when she stood up to Mr. Callahan? How does she feel about it in Chapter 18?

3. What is Miya worried about when she can't sleep the night before the barrel race? Have you ever been so worried that you couldn't sleep?

4. What happened to Miya in her very first race?

5. Does Miya regret not listening to Lisa?

6. How do Jake and Mr. Callahan try to help Miya when she returns to school? Do you think they make a difference for Miya after all of the negative comments about her run?

7. Do you think Lily intentionally broke Miya's sculpture of Dream? Why or why not?

Chapters 21-23

1. Do you think Miya overreacted to losing her sculpture? Why or why not?

2. How do Mom, Jake, Abigail, and Lisa try to support Miya?
3. On the bus, Jake says that Miya should give Lily a break. Do you agree? Why or why not?
4. How has Mr. Callahan changed by the end of Chapter 22?
5. Is it fair that Mr. O. insists that Miya complete a sculpture?
6. Why does Miya agree to try and repair the sculpture of Dream?
7. What do Lisa, Jake, and Abigail do to support Miya in Chapter 23? Find examples in the text.
8. What do Skylar and Ella attempt to do to Lily?
9. Should Miya have done what she did or walked away?

Chapters 24-Epilogue

1. Lily never apologized for how she hurt Miya, yet Dad thinks Miya should forgive her. What do you think?
2. How does Lily begin to change by the end of Chapter 24? Find examples to support your answer.
3. Compare and contrast Miya's second barrel race with her first one.
4. How has Miya changed by the end of the book? What are some of the lessons she learned?

Acknowledgments

Thank you to the following people for all of their help and support:

Editors Lindsey Maugham, Keri De Deo, Malory Wood, Claire Shepherd and especially Patricia Landy. Cover design by Deanna Estes and art by Tawni Shuler.

Thank you to Jennifer Just who patiently guided me through numerous first drafts of the book. To Janis and Ron Adams, for their ministry at Camp Wannabe and allowing me to be a small part of it. To Michelle King, storyteller, who encouraged me to tell mine.

Thank you to all the readers who patiently perused and commented on the early drafts of *Miya's Dream*: Sherry Hale, Anna Poe, Trent Reed, Jennisen Lucas, Missy Gernhart and her rodeoing daughters Cami and Gabi, Julie and Bella Linebaugh of Silver Spur Arena, and Allison Whisler of Whisler Equine Services.

I would like to express my gratitude to Becca and Brandon Tillery, and Ashley Whisler for their understanding and enthusiasm even when mine faltered. Special thanks to Alex Whisler for sharing his expertise with technology.

Finally, thank you to my best friend and husband, Von. He gave me my horse of a lifetime, Sundance, and he always finds time to ride with me.

About the Author

Cathy Ringler is a storyteller, cowgirl, and retired teacher. She lives at the foot of the beautiful Beartooth Mountains and rides in them as often as her busy schedule allows. Winner of the 2016 YA Wyoming Writer's Award, co-winner of the 2017 Elizabeth's World Kindness Writing Award, and two-time winner of the Gib Masters Journalistic Writing Award, Cathy enjoys working with youth. She has taught the Writing Workshop at Clark School, tutored students in literacy, volunteers at a horse camp for teens, and tells stories of horseback adventures at the annual Big Horn Arts Festival.

cathyringler.com

CPSIA information can be obtained
at www.ICGtesting.com
Printed in the USA
LVHW010033200620
658570LV00011B/1119